BOY BAND

OF THE APOCALYPSE

FOR MY LITTLE SISTER LOUISE – *TN*
FOR MY BIG SISTER HELEN – *DO'C*

First American Edition 2019
Kane Miller, A Division of EDC Publishing

Text copyright © Tom Nicoll, 2017
Illustrations copyright © David O'Connell, 2017
Author photograph © Chris Scott
Illustrator photograph © Paul Galbraith
Images © shutterstock.com
First published in Great Britain in 2017 by STRIPES Publishing,
an imprint of the Little Tiger Group.

For information contact:
Kane Miller, A Division of EDC Publishing
PO Box 470663
Tulsa, OK 74147-0663
www.kanemiller.com
www.edcpub.com
www.usbornebooksandmore.com

Library of Congress Control Number: 2018942390

Printed and bound in the United States of America

1 2 3 4 5 6 7 8 9 10

ISBN: 978-1-61067-830-8

BOY BAND
OF THE APOCALYPSE

APOCALIPS

TOM NICOLL

ILLUSTRATED BY
DAVID O'CONNELL

Kane Miller
A DIVISION OF EDC PUBLISHING

APOCALIPS

CHAPTER ONE

★ ★ ★

The world was about to end.

Four demonic figures slipped silently through the crowd. I blinked and three were gone, lost in the darkness, but I could still see one heading my way. Then I realized that the trap was already set – the others had split off to surround me. There was nowhere to run. I was like a wounded gazelle, cut off from the herd. Except the creatures stalking me were not lions or cheetahs. They were not of this world. They were teenage girls.

"Sam!" said Veronica, a tall, flat-nosed girl with long blond hair, appearing in front of me, blocking my path. "Didn't expect to see *you* here."

"I'm just—" I began.

"Big fan are you, Sam?" interrupted Vicky, to my left. Vicky was identical to Veronica.

"Me? No way!" I said. I tried to laugh, to make a point of how ridiculous her suggestion was, but it came out as a sort of belch instead.

"You don't have to pretend with us, Sam," said Violet, to my right, who was identical to Vicky. "It's great that you came."

"And soooo brave," said Valerie, from behind me. If you guessed that Valerie was identical to Violet, you'd be wrong. Valerie, like Vicky, was actually the spitting image of Veronica.

Obviously I'm kidding – they all looked like each other. Sometimes I just like to tell jokes when I sense that I'm in mortal danger. I think it's some kind of defense mechanism. Though obviously a terrible one. A sword or something would be much more useful.

Identical quadruplets are pretty rare as it happens.

You're more likely to be struck by lightning than to ever meet any. And in the case of the Heatherstones, you'd actually prefer that. Normally all four dressed the same, and the only way to tell them apart was by the gold name necklaces they wore. Over the years, though, I had developed a pretty reliable instinct for knowing who was who without any need for jewelry-based assistance. Another mostly useless defense mechanism. To my surprise, today they were actually dressed differently, each wearing a black T-shirt with the word APOCALIPS emblazoned on it but with the face of a different teenage boy beneath.

"None of the other boys from school would be seen dead at a boy band concert," said Veronica. "They all think Apocalips is just for girls."

"Which is *totally* unfair," said Vicky. "I don't see why boys can't enjoy them. They are a boy band after all."

"Totally," agreed Violet. "So what other girl things do you like, Sam?"

The quads burst into laughter. I would have preferred them to burst into flames. I knew I had to set the record straight quickly, or I might as well not bother turning up for school on Monday. As if it wasn't bad enough having them sitting right behind me in class the whole time.

"You've got it all wrong," I said hastily. "I'm here with my sister and her friend Amy. My parents asked me to take them."

The Heatherstones looked at each other and erupted again. "Lexi's here?" said Valerie, wiping away a tear. "Oh, Sam. Come on now, even you can come up with a better excuse than that. As if Lexi would ever come to something like this."

I knew what they meant. A boy band concert was not somewhere you'd ever expect to find my little sister. But she was here all right.

"It's true," I said. "Her friend Amy loves Apocalips, but her parents wouldn't let her go by herself. She begged Lexi to come with her, and my parents asked me to take them."

The Heatherstones had stopped laughing and were shifting restlessly, looking over their shoulders. The thought of Lexi being nearby had clearly put them on edge, as it should.

"Well, I don't see them," said Violet. "Are you sure you didn't leave them at home?"

"Yeah, he was too excited to see his idols," laughed Vicky. She pointed at the face on her T-shirt. "I bet he's a total Warren fan."

"Nah, I'd say he likes Pete," said Valerie, glancing down at her T-shirt.

"Looks more like a Donnie guy to me," chipped in Veronica.

"Oh, now I'd have said Frankie," said Violet.

The four girls looked at each other. "Steve!" they said.

"That's it, he's definitely a Steve," said Vicky.

I wasn't really sure what a Steve was, but I was desperate to get them off my back. "Lexi's just gone to the bathroom," I explained. "She'll be back any minute. Honestly, I hate Apocalips. They're terrible."

OK, so that probably wasn't a very smart thing to say. The four of them glared at me and started closing in again. No one was laughing anymore.

"What did you just say?" said Violet coldly.

"Terrible…" said Valerie as if she was turning the word over in her mouth. "He called them terrible."

"Apocalips is the greatest band of all time," said Vicky.

"I think our friend Sam needs to be taught a lesson in music appreciation," said Veronica.

I had only agreed to bring Lexi and her friend to watch the most popular boy band in the history of the universe because Mom and Dad had promised to buy me a new phone. I had known it was going to be dangerous. If word got out at school it would be first-degree humiliation – worse than getting caught eating your own boogers or getting kissed by your mom in public. But I really wanted that phone, so I had prepared myself for possible social destruction. I hadn't prepared myself for *actual* destruction.

"Step away from my brother."

Instinctively, the Heatherstones took a step backward as a grumpy-looking ten-year-old girl pushed her way through the crowd. My sister's best friend, Amy, shuffled up nervously behind her. To the untrained eye, Lexi, with her brown braids and her tiny stature, looked like the most innocent child you could ever meet. But that was a bit like mistaking a rattlesnake for a jump rope.

Lexi glared at the Heatherstones and they glared right back. But then doubt seemed to creep into the quadruplets' faces, their eyes darting between one another.

I should probably explain some things about my sister. I mean, she's great and everything – I love her to pieces. In fact I doubt most thirteen-year-old boys get along with their ten-year-old sister like I do. But Lexi has … issues. Anger-management issues. Her fuse is so short it's practically nonexistent. She's always getting herself into fights with other girls. And boys. Anyone really. It's not that she's a bad person. The opposite in fact. Most of the fights she gets into only happen because she's sticking up for someone else. She's saved my skin on more occasions than I can count.

And about those fights – the thing is, she always, *always* wins.

The standoff continued for a few more moments until darkness engulfed us completely. Seconds later the arena erupted with thousands of girls screaming their heads off.

The place lit up in a blaze of multicolored explosions and then there they were. The five members of Apocalips singing and dancing and jumping around to a song I'd heard a zillion times yet for the life of me couldn't remember the name of.

The Heatherstones, thankfully, had taken the opportunity to disappear, no doubt busy shoving their way through the crowd to get to the front. We were a long way from the stage, close to the back of the arena, in fact, so my first thought was that the more space between us and them, the better. But as the full horror of the world's number-one boy band began to play out in front of me, I began to wonder if death at the hands of the Heatherstones would have been better.

Baby, baby, baby, baby, baby
Baby, baby, baby, baby, baby
Yeah, baby, baby, baby
Baby, baby, baby, baby, baby
Baaaaaaaaaaaaby
Baby, baby, baby, baby, baby
Baby, baby, baby, baby, baby
Yeah, baby, baby, baby
Baby, baby, baby, baby, baby
Baaaaaaaaaaaaby
Baaaaaaaaaaaaby

Oh yeah, I do know this song. I think it's called "Baby."

"How do they remember all the words?" Lexi shouted in my ear, as if reading my mind.

As the song finished, giant green neon lights lit up behind the group spelling out the name **WARREN**. A muscular boy with a granite chin and a reddish-brown pompadour – a sort of handsome troll in a vest – took center stage.

"Who do you think that is?" I asked Lexi.

Lexi laughed. "I think he's called Warren."

"Ah," I said. "Was it the giant neon lettering that gave him away?"

"Just a little," said Lexi.

A thin boy sporting a ponytail and wearing skinny jeans coupled with a way-too-small T-shirt replaced Warren, blowing kisses to the crowd as the lights quickly rearranged themselves to spell out **FRANKIE**.

"Do you think that's Frankie?" I asked.

"Hard to say," said Lexi.

A scruffy-looking character with a lot of hair called **PETE** was up next. He had on a pair of ripped jeans and a tank top that looked badly in need of a wash. Actually, so did he.

Then came a particularly grim-looking boy called **DONNIE**. His hair was short and neat, black with dyed-green bangs, and his face was pale and angular. He wore a black shirt, a black suit jacket, black leather trousers and black shoes. His look was black, basically.

Last up was **STEVE**, the most clean-cut of them all, with a sweeping blond hairdo and perfect smile, wearing a light-blue shirt and tie, casual trousers, a pair of flip-flops and one of those porkpie hats. He bounced around the stage like a puppy on a bouncy castle. It was obvious from his enthusiasm that Steve was the lead singer of the band. That and the fact that he was in the middle. Even I know that the best singer always gets to go in the middle. It's boy band 101.

I could see Lexi rolling her eyes at the whole

thing. It was obvious she wanted to be here even less than I did. Her friend Amy, on the other hand, was beside herself in floods of tears. Of joy, I presumed.

"Just so you know," I said, leaning in so Lexi could hear me. "I had that all under control back there."

She didn't look convinced. "Oh, really? Because you reminded me of the animals on those nature shows that Dad likes."

"The lions?" I asked hopefully.

"No, the other ones," said Lexi. "The ones just minding their own business."

"Oh," I said, disappointed she had made the gazelle connection, too. "It never ends well for them, does it?"

"Nope," she said.

I looked up at the stage as Apocalips broke into their next number. I couldn't believe I'd have to endure two hours of this. And then have the Heatherstones tell everyone I actually enjoyed it.

But the more I watched, the more I grudgingly

had to admit that even though it wasn't my thing, the five of them were obviously talented. The lead singer, Steve, in particular had a pretty phenomenal voice.

The others weren't really in his league as singers, yet there was something about the four that drew you in somehow. Call it stage presence or charisma or the X factor or whatever, but there was something almost hypnotic about them, like you couldn't look away…

Someone tugged on my sleeve, breaking the spell.

"You know you don't have to stick around, right?" Lexi said.

"But I promised Mom and Dad…"

"You promised that you'd bring us here and bring us home. Nobody said you had to actually witness this horror show."

With the bouncy one now taking the stage for what appeared to be a solo performance, I wasn't going to need a lot of convincing. "I suppose I could go and get something to eat. If you're sure you'll be

OK," I added, prompting my sister to roll her eyes.

I left Lexi and Amy to it, after agreeing to meet up at the end of the concert by the box office. Unsurprisingly, the lines for the food stand were nonexistent, so I bought an overpriced hamburger, some overpriced fries and an overpriced cola. I had just sat down and torn off the burger wrapper when a chill went up my spine, and I felt a deep, yet familiar, sense of impending doom wash over me. I looked up. Four very mean, very angry and very identical faces were looking down on me.

"What are you doing out here?" I asked. "Shouldn't you be in there where the noise is? Music! I meant music."

The four girls exchanged glances.

"Yes, we should be…" said Valerie, through gritted teeth.

"But those ridiculous security guards thought otherwise," put in Vicky.

"Just because we were trying to get to the front," added Veronica.

"It's ridiculous," said Violet. "They can't prove that those girls didn't knock *themselves* out."

"Exactly," agreed Vicky. "Anyway, we're not allowed back in. And we're all very, very upset about that. So I guess we're going to have to find something to take out our frustrations on."

My hands were trembling so much that my burger fell to the ground with a splat. "I-i-is there even the slightest chance that won't involve me?" I stuttered.

The Heatherstones shook their heads.

APOCALIPS

CHAPTER TWO

★★★

All things considered, it could have been much worse. Sure, I was now locked inside a pitch-black storeroom, but on the plus side, I could no longer hear the music.

In the end, the Heatherstones had decided to refocus their efforts on finding a way back into the concert and not murder me just yet. Instead they locked me inside the first room they could find. Unfortunately they hadn't really been clear whether this was my entire punishment, or just the appetizer before the main course of torment. Either way, escaping seemed like a sensible idea.

I decided to call Lexi for help. Then I remembered I don't own a phone. And neither does she. That's what got me into this mess in the first place. I had been begging my parents for one for what felt like forever. When they offered me the Lexi deal, I had jumped at it. "All I have to do now is *not* end up stuck inside this room for the rest of my life," I said into the darkness.

After some fumbling, I managed to find the light switch. I could see now that the room was empty except for some shelves, a couple of cans of paint and a mop bucket. I tried to think about the situation rationally. That's what my best friend, Milo, would do. Milo was smart. He'd be able to look at the problem logically, like Sherlock Holmes or someone clever like that, and figure out an ingenious escape plan.

Let's see then: an empty room, no way out; a single light bulb, blinking dimly. The walls: cinderblocks. The floor: concrete. The door: steel and impenetrable. The shelves: wooden. The paint: brown. The bucket: missing a mop.

It all fell into place. I knew exactly what to do. **"HEEEEEELLLLLPPPP!!!!"** I yelled.

Elementary, as Holmes would say.

Unsurprisingly, no one heard me scream. I slumped down onto the cold floor and, as if it had been waiting for its cue, the light bulb blew, plunging me into darkness once again.

"Perfect," I said.

I woke up some time later to the sound of people arguing. I hadn't meant to fall asleep, but the room didn't exactly offer much in the way of entertainment. At least if the light had stayed on I could have cracked open a can of paint and spent the time watching its contents dry.

How long had I been asleep? A quick glance at my watch confirmed that I couldn't see my watch, so that didn't help. The arguing grew louder, and I realized it was coming from the other side of the far wall.

Suddenly, a single beam of light split the storeroom in two, shining through a ragged hole about the size of an apple in the wall opposite me.

How had I not noticed that? I wouldn't be adding the words "natural detective" to my list of talents anytime soon. Which left the list looking like this:

My Talents

1.

As the voices grew louder, I snuck up to the hole and peeked through. Not only did it seem I had slept long enough for the concert to have finished, but now I was looking into Apocalips's dressing room. All five members were present and not one of them looked happy.

"Forget about it. You can't leave, it's not happening," said a boy with muscles on his muscles. Warren, I remembered, thanks to those huge neon letters.

"Of course I can," said Steve, sounding and looking much less excited than the last time I saw him.

"You signed a contract, Steve," said the grim-looking one called Donnie, his voice much deeper and more serious than the others.

"So? People leave bands all the time," said Steve.

"Not *this* band," said the walking fur ball that was Pete.

I held my watch up to the light – it was 9:00 p.m. I thought about shouting to them so they could come around and let me out. Every moment I spent listening to the band squabbling in their dressing room meant another moment spent by Lexi and Amy standing around waiting for me. And Mom and Dad had made it very clear that one of the conditions for me getting my phone was bringing them home in one piece.

Instead I kept quiet. It was obvious that I was witnessing something I shouldn't be. Steve leaving the band didn't matter much to me, but even I knew this would be massive news. The papers were going to go nuts and millions of Apocalips fans would be gutted. But that wasn't the only reason why I didn't try to get their attention. I just had a strong feeling that it was best to keep silent and still.

"You signed the contract in blood," growled Donnie.

"Yeah, about that," said Steve. "That was a bit weird."

"Blood is binding," said Donnie. "Our destiny is your destiny."

"OK," sighed Steve. "See, that's another thing. When you all start talking about destinies and omens and prophecies and all that sort of thing, well, to be perfectly honest, it creeps me out. And when you talk about your plans for world domination—"

"What about our plans for world domination?" interrupted the skinny one, Frankie.

"Well, at first I was like, *Sure! That's what I want, too. I want to be part of the biggest boy band of all time.* But sometimes, I don't know… The way you guys talk, it's like you actually want to take over the world."

There was a long, awkward pause.

"Guys?" said Steve.

"We don't really want to take over the world," said Warren. "That was just a joke."

"Well … good," said Steve. "Glad to hear it."

"We want to destroy it," said Warren.

"Good, that's much… Sorry, what?"

Warren's response caught me off guard, too, so much so that I almost fell over, grabbing hold of the shelves at the last minute to stop myself and knocking a paintbrush to the floor.

"What was that?" said Frankie.

I ducked down, pressing myself firmly against the wall to keep out of sight. As much as I wanted to be found, I was pretty sure that I didn't want to be found by anyone on the other side of that wall.

"What was what?" asked Donnie.

"Thought I heard something…" Frankie's voice sounded much closer. He had to be peering in through the hole. I held my breath and didn't move.

"Can we go back to that thing you just said?" asked Steve. "About wanting to destroy the world?"

Donnie let out a sigh. "We thought you understood all this, Steve."

"We were very clear about the whole thing from the start," said Pete.

"About destroying the world?" asked Steve, sounding incredulous.

"Yes," said Pete.

"No… Not so much."

"Well," said Donnie. "What do you think about it?"

"About destroying the world?" asked Steve.

"Yes?"

"I'm not a fan."

"Oh," said Donnie. "Now that is disappointing. You happen to be very important to our plans, Steve."

I peered through the hole again to see what was going on.

A nervous Steve was backing away slowly from the others. "Hang on," he said. "You guys are actually serious about this, aren't you?"

"Yes," said Donnie. "Very much so."

"More than anything," said Pete.

"It's pretty much our only reason for being," said Frankie.

"We really, really, really, really want to destroy the world," added Warren.

Steve's mouth opened and closed a few times. "But … but … we're just a boy band," he said.

"It's always good to have side projects," said Frankie.

"Yeah, like your perfumes," said Pete.

"First of all," said Steve, "they're not perfumes. Second – you can't possibly compare my range of quality, affordable men's fragrances with the destruction of the entire planet."

"Not sure about that, mate," said Pete. "Have you actually smelled some of those things?"

Steve shot him a look. "Yes, very funny. Look, if anything this has just made my decision to leave that much easier. I can see we have some pretty major creative differences."

"You realize that we can't just let you leave, Steve," said Donnie in a tone that sent a shiver up my spine. Steve gulped, seemingly sharing the feeling.

"Oh, really?" said Steve, puffing out his chest in a way that I think was meant to make him look brave but seemed to only amplify his fear. "And I suppose you all are going to stop me?"

"If we have to," said Warren, pounding his fist into his palm.

"Our plans have been in motion for a long, long time," said Donnie. "We're too close now to see them ruined by some over-ambitious fifteen-year-old. Now is not the time for us to take risks. And letting you go would be a risk. You know too much."

"First time anyone's ever accused me of that," said Steve, smiling nervously. "So what," he said, forcing a laugh as his bandmates drew closer. "You're just going to beat me up? Is that the plan?"

There was no reply from Donnie, Frankie, Pete or Warren. But they didn't pile in to beat him up. Instead they joined hands around Steve.

"What are you—" Before Steve could utter another word, the hands of his bandmates ignited. Flames began to shoot out of them, bouncing back and forth between each member. They seemed random at first, always narrowly missing Steve himself, but quickly it began to take shape. A molten sphere was forming, encasing Steve in a fiery prison.

I watched in horror, scarcely able to believe what I was seeing. Even through the gap the heat was almost unbearable. Steve was just a faint silhouette now through the flames. His screams were muffled, drowned out by the roar of the fire. Finally there was a flash and the fireball was gone, and Steve along with it.

I stumbled backward, knocking over the paint cans and yelping as my right foot landed in the mop bucket, and I tumbled to the ground.

Way to go, Sam! I thought as I scrambled to my feet.

"There's someone in there," said Frankie. "I *knew* I heard something. They must have seen us through the hole."

"The hole that Warren thought it would be funny to make by putting his fist through the wall," said Frankie.

"It *was* funny," said Warren, laughing to himself.

"Stop wasting time," said Donnie. "Get them!"

I rushed toward the door. In my desperation I tried the handle and … it opened.

Yeah. Probably should have tried that to begin with.

I burst out of the room and bolted down the corridor, skidding straight into the wall of teenage girls making their way out of the building. I let myself get swept into their path.

I glanced over my shoulder just as they emerged into the crowd – four angry and possibly supernatural young men looking to do who knows what to me. Had they seen my face? It was pretty dark in the storeroom, but who knew what these guys were capable of.

"It's them!" shouted an excited voice, and a hundred or so girls turned to look.

The next moment the crowd swarmed on Donnie, Frankie, Pete and Warren like locusts. The four remaining members of Apocalips didn't stand a chance. My ears ringing from the screaming, I pushed my way through the crowd and headed toward the box office where Lexi and Amy and I had agreed to meet. They weren't there.

"Come on, where are you?" I muttered. "I'm in danger of being exterminated by a boy band here!"

Worried Amy might have made a dash for the band, I turned back toward the mass of girls. But then I saw them. They were standing at one of the concession stands that seemed to be selling pretty much anything you could think of putting an Apocalips logo on. I rushed over.

"Where have you been?" asked Lexi, looking slightly startled by my sudden appearance.

"Where have I been?" I said. "Where have *you* been? I said meet me at the box office, remember? We need to go. Now!"

"Sorry. We just…" said Lexi, sounding slightly shifty. "Um, it doesn't matter. Come on, Amy."

"Hang on," replied Amy. "Just let me get my stuff." She picked up several large bags, each packed full of merchandise.

"They're all yours?" I asked, snatching up a couple more. "How could you afford all that?"

"Mom gave me her credit card in case there was an emergency," she said. "Some of this stuff you can only buy at the events. I'd call that an emergency, wouldn't you?"

Of course I wouldn't, but there was no time to argue as I hurried Lexi and Amy through the main doors. For the first time that night, luck was on my side. Our bus had just pulled up across the street. And as there were now more girls heading back into the building than out of it, having heard that their idols were doing an impromptu meet and greet, we had no problem getting on.

I didn't speak a word on the bus ride home. Amy spent the whole journey excitedly recounting the entire concert to Lexi as if she hadn't been there. I was too busy keeping an eye out for anyone who looked like they might be able to fry us to death. I didn't think the band had spotted me making my getaway, but after what I had seen them do to Steve, I couldn't take anything for granted. It wouldn't have surprised me if they'd pulled up alongside the bus on broomsticks.

We saw Amy and her bags safely home and decided against sticking around for the argument with her mom about what constituted an emergency. Once I was finally convinced we weren't being followed, I decided to tell Lexi what I had seen.

"Lexi, about tonight," I said as we made our way along our street. "I need to tell you something…"

"Yeah, what's going on with you," she said. "You've been acting really oddly since the concert."

"I saw something, Lexi," I said. "Something … incredible. I … I can't really explain it…"

Lexi nodded. "I know exactly what you mean."

I screwed up my face. "You do?"

"Yeah," she said. "It's weird, I never thought I'd like Apocalips. But as the night went on … I sort of got lost in it all. You know, they're actually not that bad. In fact, they're really kind of amazing."

My stomach suddenly felt very uneasy. Then I saw something in her hand. A bag. She had been carrying it earlier, but I'd assumed it was another one of Amy's.

"What's in that?" I asked.

"Oh, this… It's silly really," she said, blushing. My sister never blushed. She pulled out an Apocalips T-shirt featuring a picture of the group jumping for no reason in particular. "I got it while I was waiting for you. You still haven't told me where you were, by the way."

I had always been close to my sister. We didn't normally keep secrets from each other. But this wasn't a normal night and something deep inside was telling me that Lexi wasn't the right person to tell my story to.

I'd have to find someone else.

APOCALIPS

CHAPTER THREE

★★★

My parents were next on the list. I tried to speak to them as soon as I got home, but I couldn't get a word in with Lexi gushing over how much she loved Apocalips now. By the time she had finished, they were too tired to talk.

"But Mom, Dad," I said as they headed upstairs to bed. "I really need to speak to you."

Mom yawned. "Don't worry, Sam, we haven't forgotten about your phone. We can talk about it tomorrow."

"Good night, son," said Dad.

I decided to go to bed myself, setting the alarm

on my watch to make sure I was up before my sister.

When my alarm sounded the next morning it felt like I'd hardly slept. I'd tossed and turned all night, the events of the concert running through my head in a loop. Still, I dragged myself out of bed, tiptoed past Lexi's room and downstairs to the kitchen.

"Morning, Sam," said Mom, placing a couple of cups of coffee on the table. "Well, your sister seemed to enjoy herself last night, didn't she? It's so nice to see her interested in something other than fighting for a change. Thank you for taking her and Amy. I suppose you want to talk about phones now?"

I shook my head. "Maybe another time," I said, looking around the room for signs of my sister. "Is Lexi still in bed?"

"She was up ages ago," replied Mom. "She's over at Amy's listening to Apocalips records."

There was a grunt from the other end of the table. "Kids don't listen to records anymore, Martha," said Dad, from behind a huge newspaper. "It's all compact discs now."

"Actually, it's not even that anymore," I said.

"Oh, right, yes… It's all computers now, isn't it? Free-MPs and Ear-Pods and what have you. Webs and nets and clouds and things."

"Yeah, that's it, Dad," I said. My parents didn't really have a clue about … well, anything modern really. They're basically the most boring people you've ever met. They met at Accountant School (or whatever it's called) and then went to work for the same firm – *Stanley, Stanley, Hanson and Stanley*, where they've worked for fifteen years. They both dress in gray suits, both have short gray hair and both wear gray spectacles. My dad has a beard and a bit of a gut gained from what he calls OBC – Office Birthday Cakes. That's probably the most exciting thing I can think of to say about them.

So yeah, they were boring and sensible. But right now, boring and sensible was good.

"So how was it for you then?" asked Mom. "Not too awful, I hope?"

"It was fine," I said. "Except for the bit at the end when the band killed one of their members because he wouldn't help them destroy the world."

Mom sipped her coffee.

Dad tutted. "The things that pass for music these days."

Mom smiled at Dad. "It was different in our day," she said. "People just went out to dance and have a good time, not to kill people and destroy the world."

"That's how your mother and I met," said Dad, gazing at Mom over the top of the paper.

"What, when you were killing people and destroying the world?" I asked.

"No, I meant dancing," said Dad.

"Hang on," I said. "I thought you two met when you were learning to be accountants?"

Mom and Dad stared at me, blinking a few times, before Mom blurted out, "Yes, of course we did! But it was at a … a concert. That's where we met. Your father and I. We met at a concert … at college."

Dad nodded in agreement.

I might have questioned them further to find out why they were acting so shiftily, but there was a far more serious issue to deal with.

"Can we get back to Apocalips wanting to destroy the world," I said. "I saw them make someone disappear in a big ball of fire."

"Oh now, Sam, don't be so silly," said Mom. "It would have just been a special effect."

"In their dressing room?" I said. I could still feel the heat from the fire and hear Steve's desperate yells through the roar of the flames. It was no special effect.

"Dressing room?" said Mom. "And how could you possibly have seen inside their dressing room?"

I paused. If I told my parents how I came to witness what had happened, I'd be admitting to not staying with Lexi and Amy as I had promised. And that'd mean bye-bye, phone.

On the other hand, a phone wouldn't be much use if the world was destroyed.

"Never mind," I said, realizing I was talking to the wrong people. Just what exactly did I expect two accountants to be able to do, anyway? What use was the ability to manage spreadsheets going to be against the forces of evil? No, there was only one person who could help. But would he believe me?

He was waiting by the swings, the boy with the cornrows in his hair, wearing a thick padded jacket even though it was June. Not actually on the swings – Milo tended to avoid … well, everything really. One of the perks of being my best friend was that the Heatherstones tormented him, too. But being so small also made him a target for the other kids at school. No matter what he did, he would always get laughed at for it. So after a while he just stopped doing anything if he thought someone might see him. Even now, with the park completely empty, he wasn't risking the swings. Still, he was my best friend and the smartest person I knew.  Convincing him I was telling the truth was going to be hard.

"So what do you think?" I asked, after explaining what had happened.

"Sounds plausible to me," said Milo.

OK, maybe not *that* hard.

I screwed up my face. "Plausible? That a boy band killed one of their own and plans to destroy the world? I was there and even I don't think it sounds plausible."

Milo shrugged. "To be honest, I'm more surprised this doesn't happen all the time."

"What are you talking about?"

"Well, I've long suspected that all boy bands must be evil on some level. It's why the music they make is so good."

That caught me off guard. "You like the music?"

Milo looked at me with surprise. "What's not to like? Strong melodies, memorable hooks, and who doesn't love a good key change? And you can dance to it."

"You don't dance," I said.

"Yeah, but it's nice to have the option, isn't it?" he said. "Anyway, back to my point. If you accept that all boy bands are evil, which I think we can say they definitely are, then it all comes down to *how* evil they are. Because some boy bands will be less evil than others. Like releasing bad cover versions of classic songs or bringing out a greatest hits compilation when they've only released one album. Despicable stuff to be sure but hardly full-on evil.

"Then you'll get what I like to call mid-range evil," he continued. "This level would include things like being rude to fans, getting into fights with photographers or stealing ice cream trucks – that kind of thing. And then above that you'd come to the bands at the high end of the evil scale. The ones that want to bring about the end of days. I'd guess that over the course of human history, there's probably been in the region of twenty thousand boy bands."

I considered this. I suppose when you took into consideration all the bands that never made it, it seemed like a reasonable guess. "OK," I said. "Go on."

"Which means that even if only one percent of all boy bands were max-grade evil, we're still talking around two hundred that wanted nothing more than to bring about the Apocalypse. It's a terrifying thought."

"It's an insane thought," I said.

Milo nodded. "Exactly."

"I really don't think it's as high as that," I added.

He wasn't about to be discouraged. "I'm telling you, Sam," he said, looking past me. "Some boy bands just want to watch the world burn."

"Well, let's just focus on this one for now, shall we?" I said. "We have to do something."

"Like what?" he asked.

"I don't know," I said. "Go to the police?"

Milo shook his head. "No point," he said. "They'd never believe you."

"You did," I said.

"Yeah, but that's only because I know you'd never be able to come up with a story as nuts as that by yourself."

"Right," I said. "Thanks. So it's up to us then."

"Looks like it," said Milo.

"You got any ideas?" I asked.

"Tons," he said. "But none about solving this particular problem."

We stayed in the park for another hour, trying to come up with a plan. This mostly involved me watching Milo scribble away in the notebook he always carried with him. Every so often he would frown, mutter something under his breath then tear the page out, roll it into a ball and toss it into a nearby trash can. When he had come to the last page, this is what we were left with:

| Ideas to stop Apocalips from destroying the planet |
| 1. |

"It's not a very big list," said Milo.

"No," I agreed. "Maybe we should sleep on it."

"It's definitely not big enough to sleep on."

"Very funny," I said.

"OK, I'll go home and work on it," said Milo. "I think better in my room anyway. I'm not as worried about Heatherstones randomly showing up there as I am, well, everywhere else."

The walk home didn't provide me with any extra inspiration. As I shut the front door I could hear what sounded like crying coming from upstairs. I met my mom on the landing.

"Mom, what's going on?" I asked.

"It's your sister," she said.

I began to panic, horrible thoughts racing through

my mind. Lexi never cried, apart from when she was younger and Mom and Dad refused to let her watch kung fu DVDs. "What's wrong with Lexi?"

"She's had some bad news."

At that moment, the door to Lexi's room swung open, to reveal my sister standing there in

the Apocalips T-shirt she had bought the night before. Her face was red and puffy, with tears streaming down her cheeks.

"Lexi, what is it?"

"Oh, Sam," she said. "They just announced it."

"Announced what?" I asked.

"It's Steve," she said.

Steve, I thought. *So they know. They all know now.*

"What about him?" I asked, still needing to hear someone else say it.

"He's gone," she said. "He's quit the band."

APOCALIPS

CHAPTER FOUR

★★★

It seemed like a lifetime ago that my biggest worry had been the Heatherstones telling everyone that I had been at the Apocalips concert. They didn't even show up for school on Monday. In fact, none of the girls did. Some of the boys were missing, too. Lexi hadn't even left her bed that morning. The news of Steve's departure from the band had hit their fans hard.

Departure – that was what they were calling it. The "official" story was that Steve had left to start a solo career and that the rest of the group wished him all the best in his future endeavors. I couldn't help think that as upset as the fans were, they'd be a lot more upset if they knew what had really happened to Steve.

I had just taken my seat when our teacher Mr. Humphries showed up, looking even more annoyed than he usually did on a Monday morning.

"All right, everyone," he said, letting out a sigh. "The headmistress has just received word from the Department for Education. Apparently levels of absence are through the roof at every school in the country. The prime minister, no doubt on orders from his two daughters, has just declared a week of national mourning."

"What does that mean, sir?" I asked.

"It means the world has gone mad," said Mr. Humphries. "All this because some little poser has left another group of posers. Still, on the bright side, it also means we all get a week off. Your parents have been informed by email ... so off you go then."

Cheers went up around the class. Moments later Milo and I strolled out of the school gate as Mr. Humphries flew past in his old Mini. It was probably the only time I had ever seen him with a smile on his face.

"Can you believe what they're saying?" I asked Milo.

"It's the perfect cover story," he replied. "A boy band member leaving to start their solo career is like someone going into witness protection. Ninety-nine percent of the time it's like they just drop off the face of the earth. The only difference is that unlike people in witness protection, nobody ever bothers to go looking for them."

"So those ... whatever they are, just get away with killing him?" I said. "We need to stop them."

"About that," said Milo. "I think I might have an idea."

I stopped walking. "Really? Milo, that's great!"

From Milo's expression, he didn't seem to share my enthusiasm. "Uh, yeah," he mumbled. "I don't suppose you happened to catch the news this morning?"

I shook my head. I had spent so long trying to convince Lexi to get up that I'd barely had time to grab a slice of toast before I left for school.

"Why?" I asked.

"Oh, no reason."

"So what's the plan?"

"It's probably best I explain this at my house," said Milo. "But you're not going to like it."

"I don't like it," I said, after Milo had shown me the clip in his room.

"I thought as much," said Milo. "But trust me, this is the only way."

"There has to be another way," I said, hearing the desperation in my own voice.

"There isn't," said Milo. "I wish there was but there's not. This is our one shot at getting close to the band and finding out what they're planning."

But we weren't just talking about me being close to the band. We were talking about me being *in* the band. I held my head in my hands.

"Play it again," I said.

Milo clicked on the link. Four sad-looking boys appeared on the computer screen. They were sitting on a long couch holding hands. At the end of the couch was an empty space.

"As you all know," began Warren, who was so big he took up most of the couch by himself, "Apocalips has lost a huge part of itself. Five have become four. Steve was … I mean *is* a brilliant performer who touched all our hearts. We have nothing but love and respect for him, and all that he has done for us."

"While we wish Steve the best of luck for the future," said Donnie, in that deep, monotonous voice of his, "we as a group must look to our own future. There was never any question that Apocalips would live on. We live for our fans. They are what give us strength. We feed off their love."

I couldn't help giving a shudder at this.

Frankie spoke next, crossing his skinny legs. "We thought about carrying on, just the four of us. But then we came up with a better idea. You see, someone once decided to take a chance on all of us. So we thought to ourselves: what if we gave someone else a shot? Just like the one we had."

"That's right," said Pete, from somewhere behind a great mass of straggly hair. "Apocalips is recruiting. One lucky young man is going to have the opportunity to join us. Auditions will be taking place this Saturday at the National Arena for TV Talent Shows. If you think you have what it takes to be the next member of Apocalips, and you're aged between thirteen and sixteen, then you'd better make sure you're there."

"We're looking for someone who can sing," said Warren.

"And dance," said Donnie.

"Who has something special about him," added Frankie.

"And won't mind putting up with us," said Pete as the others laughed.

"If that sounds like you," they said together, pointing toward the screen, "then we can't wait for you to join us."

The clip ended and I turned to Milo. "For argument's sake," I said, "let's say that this isn't a dumb idea. I mean, just to be clear – it definitely is a dumb idea. But if we just pretend for a minute that it's not, how on earth am I going to get picked? I can't sing or dance. And there's nothing special about me."

"What are you talking about?" asked Milo. "You've got a great singing voice. What about that Christmas show you were in a few years ago. You were amazing in that."

I had to rack my brains to remember what he was talking about. "You don't mean the school Nativity?" I asked. "That was when we were babies. And I didn't sing in it. I played the donkey – the back part."

"Yeah, but you had great stage presence," said Milo. "That's really what they're looking for with these things."

"They're looking for a donkey that can't sing or dance?" I asked.

Milo shrugged. "You'd be surprised with some of these boy bands," he said. "Besides, you're forgetting one thing."

"What's that?"

"Auditions aren't till Saturday," said Milo. "And we have the week off. That gives us five days to turn you into a first-rate boy band member."

"Why does it have to be me?" I said. "What about you? Why don't you do it?"

Milo looked at me as if I'd told him I was seeing one of the Heatherstones.

"Because," he said slowly, "there isn't a lot of call among boy bands for short, shy, ugly kids."

"You're not ugly," I said. "Short and shy definitely. But not ugly."

"Thanks," he said, looking a little embarrassed. "Unfortunately, short and shy are enough to rule me out. It has to be you, Sam."

I sighed. I knew he was right. The fate of the world depended on me making the band. And then somehow finding a way to foil their evil plans. It was a lot to ask of a donkey.

APOCALIPS

CHAPTER FIVE

★ ★ ★

I nipped home to drop off my stuff, change out
of my school clothes and grab a bit of lunch, then
headed back to Milo's house to come up with a plan
to get me into Apocalips. When I got there it was
clear Milo had already made a start. His desk was
overflowing with piles of paper with his scribblings
all over them, along with a pile of old boy band CDs
he'd managed to get hold of from somewhere. An
Apocalips music video was paused on his computer
screen. I had seen it before. It was the one where
the band raced each other around a parking lot in
shopping carts for reasons that aren't quite clear.

"You know those carts aren't even real," said Milo casually. "It's all done with computers. Four million they spent to get them looking that realistic."

"Why didn't they just use real shopping carts?" I asked.

Milo shrugged. "No idea. Anyway, I've been researching boy bands," he said, waving at his desk. "And I've been able to boil down every boy band member to the following formula."

Milo handed me a sheet of paper.

$$Q = S \times D \times H$$

I looked at Milo blankly. "What?"

"Q means quality," said Milo. "Now, quality is determined by three factors – singing, dancing and haircut."

"Haircut?"

"That's right," said Milo. "The good news is that you don't need to have top marks in all three, but you definitely need at least one in your favor."

"Haircut?" I repeated.

"We'll get to that," said Milo. "But first we'd better start with singing. So can you hold a tune?"

I picked up a CD from the pile. "Like this?" I asked.

Milo frowned. "We haven't got time for jokes. Can you sing or not?"

"Not," I said.

Milo didn't seem to find this information worrying. "Well, let's just hear what we're dealing with. How about we start with one of Apocalips's most well-known songs: 'Where's My Girl Gone?' You know it?"

"Never heard of it," I said. It began to dawn on me just how difficult this was going to be.

Milo remained calm and handed me another sheet of paper. "I thought you might say that. There's the lyrics."

1st Verse:

I got to school, it was five to nine

Looked for my baby, she's oh so fine.
Couldn't see her, she wasn't there
I hate my life, it's so unfair.

Chorus:

Where's my girl gone, she be gone?
Have you seen her, my precious one?
Where's my girl gone, is that her there?
No, that's just me crying on the stair.

2nd Verse:

Lunchtime comes, she's not around
So I'm eating macaroni by the pound.
Dessert is pudding, sticky toffee
Without you girl, I'm in agony.

Repeat Chorus

3rd Verse:

It's home time now and I'm still alone,
There ain't no texts on my mobile phone.
Called by your house, just to vanquish my fears
But your dad said you'd been dead ten years.

Repeat Chorus x 3

"Wow," I said.

"I know, right?" said Milo. "It's like a twist ending. You think his girlfriend is just off school or something, but actually she's been dead all along. So has he been dating a ghost? Really makes you think, that one."

He was right about that. "It makes me think it's terrible," I said. "Because it is."

Milo looked at me as if I was the one that had lost it. "It won a ton of songwriting awards," he said. "It's considered a modern-day classic."

"It's not really my thing," I said.

"And what is your *thing*?" asked Milo, sounding annoyed.

I looked at him blankly. I didn't have a thing. All I could offer was a shrug.

"Exactly," said Milo. "So you're going to sing it?"

I nodded.

Milo played the song a couple of times more to drum it into my head. Then he put on just the brooding, orchestral instrumental track.

"Over to you," he said.

I got as far as the end of the first line when Milo cut me off.

"OK," he said, frowning. "So singing isn't going to be your thing."

I could feel my cheeks burning. "Was it really that bad?"

Milo took a long time to consider his reply. "I… It was… Look, I'm sorry, but you have to promise me that you will never inflict that upon another living being for as long as you live."

I started laughing but quickly stopped when I realized Milo wasn't kidding.

"Er … all right," I agreed.

"Good," he said, massaging his forehead. "Seriously, how come I didn't know you were that bad at singing?"

"Well, I've never heard you singing either, so I guess we must be going to different karaoke bars," I said sarcastically. "Now, can we get back to figuring out how to turn me into a pop star?"

For the first time I saw genuine concern on Milo's face. I could tell it was dawning on him how hopeless things were.

"The singing is going to be a problem," said Milo. "I'm going to need some time to think about how we get around that. In the meantime let's concentrate on your dancing. How's that? It can't possibly be worse than your singing."

"I haven't done a lot," I said.

"What have you done?"

I thought about it. "There was my aunt's wedding a few months back. I danced at that."

Milo leaned forward eagerly. "Yeah? And how did it go?"

I looked down at my feet. "Well, we haven't really spoken to my aunt since," I said. "But I did hear that my cousin Lucy is due to get the casts off any week now."

Milo gulped. "Here," he said, handing me another piece of paper from one of the piles. "This is a simple dance routine I found on the internet."

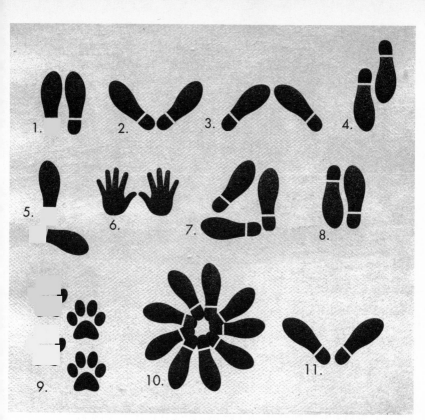

"Er, thanks," I said.

"I think it's pretty self-explanatory," said Milo.

I stared at it for a long time. I thought about Milo's formula again. Quality = Singing x Dancing x Haircut. You didn't have to be as clever as Milo to know that if any of those values happens to equal zero, then you still end up with zero.

"We're in a lot of trouble," I said.

APOCALIPS

CHAPTER SIX

★ ★ ★

I left Milo's shortly after that. I made up an excuse that I wanted to go home and check on Lexi, who had still been in bed when I had gone home earlier. I could tell Milo didn't believe me, but he didn't try to stop me either. He said he would figure out what to do about my singing and told me to focus on my dancing for now. But I think we both knew the truth. I was as hopeless at dancing as I was at singing.

Well, all right, maybe not quite that bad, but I was still awful, and there was no way I was going to be able to dance my way into a boy band by Saturday. I had to admit, there was a moment or two when I allowed myself to think that my moment was finally here. My one chance in the spotlight. I'd get to be the hero. Infiltrate an evil boy band, foil their plans and save the world. And then I remembered how useless I was at all this.

My problem is I watch too many films and read too many books about amazing kids who discover amazing talents and have amazing adventures and accomplish amazing things. I should know that's just make-believe. Not every kid gets to be like that.

As I turned into my street, I realized I hadn't passed a single person on the way home. I had been too busy feeling sorry for myself to think much of it, but now it felt a bit creepy. It was like walking through a ghost town, except without the ghosts.

Then I saw them. Four identical blond girls, dressed entirely in black, marching toward me.

I began to walk faster, hoping I would make it to my house before they made it to me. But obviously I'm not that lucky. I was about two doors away when I felt a cold hand on my shoulder.

"Might have known we'd see you out and about," said Veronica. Like her sisters, she wore a floor-length black satin dress, with a black veil covering her face. Normally I'd be grateful not to have to look at the Heatherstones' faces, but today it felt like I had stumbled into the middle of a funeral. I could only hope it wasn't mine.

"Enjoying our time off, are we?" asked Violet, her veil unable to hide the seething look on her face.

"Er … yes?" I said. It didn't seem likely that a right answer existed here.

"You're loving this, aren't you?" said Vicky. "Maybe I should wipe that smile off your face."

Fortunately for me, the other three restrained her.

"It's not appropriate for people to be out enjoying themselves," said Valerie. "The world is in mourning. It's suffered a huge loss."

It was at that moment I became aware that the Heatherstones were no longer the only girls around. Three more had appeared at the top of the street, marching together in the same black dresses and veils. Directly across the road, another squad looked to be interrogating a couple of extremely nervous-looking boys.

COWELL RD

"What's going on?" I asked.

"For some reason, not everyone seems to get the significance of what's happened," said Violet.

"So we're helping them understand," said Veronica, a twisted smile forming on her lips. "We're encouraging people to take this time to go home, be with their loved ones and reflect upon recent events."

"And what if they don't want to do that?" I asked.

"Then we let them reflect upon Vicky and see how she affects them," said Valerie.

"I can be very affecting," she said, waving her fist.

"You can't just stop people going out," I said, torn between not wanting to give in to this madness and realizing that, as terrible as my dancing was, Vicky Heatherstone breaking my legs wasn't going to help matters.

Well, actually, it might. My dancing really was bad.

"Don't think of it as us stopping you from

72

going out," said Veronica.

"Think of it as us forcing you to stay in," said Violet.

"That's the same thing," I said. "People have a right to go outside."

"Sam, what's wrong?"

I turned my head and a sense of relief washed over me. It was Lexi. The only known antidote to a Heatherstone.

"Your brother is refusing to pay his respects," said Valerie.

"Lexi, these nutters are trying to force everyone to stay inside," I answered at the same time as Valerie.

Lexi's face darkened. "That's not on," she said.

"Exactly," I said, folding my arms and grinning. It was time to say goodbye to the Heatherstones.

None of them moved. And for some reason, they were smiling back at me. Something felt very off here. I looked at my sister. She had a distant look on her face, almost like she was looking right through me. I had a feeling I wasn't going to like what was coming next.

"Lexi," I said, swallowing a large lump in my throat. "Why are you wearing that black dress?"

"Come on, Sam," she said. "We can do this the easy way or the hard way."

"Lexi… What are you…? You can't be involved in this!"

"Sounds like the hard way to me," said Vicky.

From the corner of my eye I noticed that Lexi was carrying something in her hands. Something large… Something brown… Something sack like…

And then everything went dark.

APOCALIPS

CHAPTER SEVEN

★★★

I didn't want it to come to this, but I had been left with no choice.

"Mom, Dad, Lexi put me in a sack, dragged me up to my room and dumped me there."

That's right: I told on her.

Mom and Dad were sitting in the living room tapping away at their laptops. After the week of mourning for Steve had been announced, their firm had decided to let parents work from home.

"Is that true, Lexi?" asked Mom, looking up from her screen.

"Yes," said Lexi, sounding a bit bored.

"Oh," said Mom. "Well, don't do that again."

"OK," Lexi said, getting up from the sofa. "Now, can I go? The Heatherstones are waiting for me." Before Mom could answer she was out of the room. I heard the front door slamming behind her.

I looked at my parents in disgust.

"Is that it?" I shouted. "Is that all you're going to say to her?"

"Oh, Sam. I'm sure she was just having a bit of fun," said Mom.

"A bit of fun? **SHE DRAGGED ME UP THE STAIRS IN A SACK!**"

"Girls will be girls," said Dad, as if this was supposed to make sense.

"You're right, Sam," said Mom, sounding a bit more sympathetic. "She shouldn't have done it. I'll have a talk with Lexi later. But I mean, look, you're fine and I'm sure it was the other girls daring her. We're just so relieved to see Lexi making new friends. We don't want to ruin this for her. And those Heatherstone girls are so lovely."

I almost fell over. "What? The  Heatherstones? Have you gone mad?"

"They gave us some nice armbands earlier," said Mom, pointing to the black elastic band around her arm with the word "Steve" stitched in white thread. "Your dad loves his."

"I'm using it as a pen holder," said Dad, pointing at his left arm. Sure enough, at least twenty pens were being held in place by the band.

"Did you have fun at Milo's?" asked Mom, changing the subject.

"No … not really," I said.

I moved over to the window and watched as my sister joined her new friends outside. They were looking up and down the street, probably keeping their eyes peeled for anyone else who dared to leave their home. I just couldn't understand how Lexi could have turned on me like that. And I couldn't stop thinking about that hollowed-out look she had in her eyes. It was almost like she wasn't even there.

"Why not?" asked Mom, interrupting my thoughts.

"Why not what?" I said.

"Why didn't you have fun at Milo's?"

Coming back from Milo's I had almost talked myself out of going to audition, but now I knew I had no choice. Whatever was going on with Lexi, I knew it had something to do with Apocalips, and I was pretty sure it had nothing to do with their music. I could feel my cheeks burning as I realized I was actually going to go through with Milo's insane plan. But worse than that – I'd have to tell my mom and dad. I took a deep breath.

"If you must know," I said. "We were practicing for the Apocalips audition."

My parents' mouths dropped open. "Milo's going to audition?" asked Mom. "The boy who never speaks when I'm in the same room as him?"

"He's a bit small to be in a boy band, isn't he?" said Dad.

"I don't think there's a height restriction, Dad,"

I said. "It's not the fire department."

"Ooh, Fire Department," said Mom, pretending to swoon. "Now there was a good boy band."

I shook my head. "Anyway, no, I didn't mean Milo," I said. "I meant me. I'm going to audition."

If the thought of Milo auditioning for a boy band had stunned them, it was nothing compared to the idea that their own son would be. I had never known silence like it.

My mom spoke first.

"You're … auditioning? For the band?"

"Yes," I said.

"You?" asked Dad.

"Yes."

"In a band?" said Mom.

"Yes."

"Our son?" asked Dad.

"Yes."

"As in you?" said Mom.

This went on for about

five minutes. Eventually I snapped.

"Is it really so hard to imagine me being in a band?"

Mom and Dad looked at each other.

"Yes!" they said.

"Thank you very much," I said.

"What we mean," said Mom, "is that … well, it's just … you singing… Do you remember that time we went caroling?"

As much as I tried to block out that memory, I did remember. It had been three years ago, but I'd never forget the looks on those poor people's faces. "Yeah, but—"

"Property prices still haven't recovered around here, you know," said Dad.

"And then there's your dancing…" continued Mom.

"We were very lucky your aunt agreed to settle out of court," said Dad.

"All right, fine, I get it," I shouted. "I'm no good."

Mom reached out and took hold of my hand.

"No, sweetheart, it's not that. It's just … your talents might not be on the stage, that's all."

"Yeah?" I said, pulling my hand away. "So what are my talents then?"

"Well, you can fit inside a sack comfortably," said Dad, smiling.

"Harold!" said Mom, pulling his armband and letting it go, causing a loud smack as his pens flew everywhere.

"Ouch!" cried Dad. "I was joking. You've got lots of talents. You're good with the … you know … you're great at … um … there's uh… Martha, help me out?"

Mom rolled her eyes. "Well … you've always been good at…"

I let out a sigh.

"Lots of things!" said Mom quickly. "You're good at lots of things. Not necessarily one thing in particular. You haven't found your specialty yet, that's all."

"Exactly," said Dad. "You're a jack-of-all-trades really."

"But not singing or dancing," I said.

"Well, no, not those trades," admitted Dad.

"Anyway, I didn't know you were a fan of Apocalips," said Mom. "I don't understand why you'd even want to be in the band. And the music industry is no place for a young person. It'll eat you up and spit you out."

"What would you know about it?" I asked.

Mom turned away. "Well … er … nothing, of course," she said. "But you hear about it, don't you. On the TV and in magazines. And besides, weren't you telling us yesterday they wanted to take over the world?"

"Destroy the world, actually," I said. "They want to destroy the world. And that's exactly why I'm auditioning. To stop them."

"Right … right…" said Dad, giving me a wink. "Nothing to do with all those screaming girls then?"

I gave a sigh and headed up to my room.

I kneeled on the end of my bed and looked out

—

of the window onto the street where my little sister was ordering a couple of small boys back to their house. Ever since the concert it was like her mind had been altered. I had already seen what Apocalips were capable of. Mind control didn't seem too much of a stretch. Whatever it was, I knew that wasn't the real Lexi. I had to get her back. And save the world.

A jack-of-all-trades.

A master of none.

But still, I had to try.

APOCALIPS

CHAPTER EIGHT

★ ★ ★

I spent the rest of the afternoon perfecting my dancing. By the end of the day I had succeeded. It was perfectly dreadful.

That night, before bed, I decided to spend some time investigating the band itself. I had to know what I was up against. Lexi had come home with a book on Apocalips that she had borrowed from Amy, so I had swiped it when she wasn't looking. It was called **Apocalicious – The 100% Unauthorized History of the Biggest Band in the World.**

Of course I wasn't going to read the whole thing, so I flicked to a section called "Quick Profiles."

DONNIE

With his brooding good looks, pale complexion and general air of mysteriousness, Donnie is Apocalips's unofficial leader. Considered the most serious of the group, Donnie's work ethic is what many believe has led the band to greatness.

Likes: Poetry, darkness, books about vampires.
Dislikes: Sunlight.

WARREN

The bad boy of the group! While he's generally loveable, Warren is known for having a short fuse and regularly gets into brawls. We've all heard stories about rock bands throwing TVs out of the window. Warren once threw a rock band out of the window.

Likes: Video games, action films.
 Dislikes: Romcoms.

FRANKIE

Frankie is a self-confessed health nut. Always on the lookout for the latest fad diets, nothing pleases him more than shedding an extra pound or ten.

Likes: Dieting.
Dislikes: Cake.

PETE

Disorganized, messy and funny are the three words that come to mind when people think of Pete. His face always hidden behind his enormous head of hair, perhaps Pete's most impressive skill is his ability to see where he's going!

Likes: Not having to tidy up.
Dislikes: Tidying, combs.

STEVE

The lead singer of the group, Steve was famously the last member to join Apocalips. According to their manager, Nigel Cruul, the group spent almost a year looking for the missing piece of the puzzle, eventually discovering Steve busking in the London Underground. "The rest is history," said Cruul.

Likes: Singing, dancing, speaking to fans.
Dislikes: Marmite, war, bad vibes.

"Well, that was helpful," I said to myself, slamming the book shut.

I had hoped to meet up with Milo the following morning to get some advice. I was clearly getting nowhere practicing alone. But when I looked out of my window, it was obvious I wasn't going anywhere. The Apocalytes had trebled the number of street patrols. I had about as much chance of making it to Milo's as I did of making the band.

Luckily they hadn't taken down the internet, so we were still able to video chat.

"It's ridiculous," said Milo, talking about the blockades. "According to Apocalips message boards, they're planning on keeping this up till Saturday."

"The day of the auditions," I said.

"Exactly," he said. "By then they'll be more bothered about seeing the new guy than missing the old one."

I told him about Lexi. He didn't seem that surprised.

"Well, after what you saw them do to Steve, we have to think about what other kinds of magic they can do," said Milo. "Hypnosis or mind control could sure come in handy if you're trying to destroy the earth."

Milo was right. But if it was that easy, why didn't Apocalips just use their powers to control armies or world leaders? Teenage girls didn't seem like the most obvious target. And how exactly did stopping kids leaving their homes for a week lead to the destruction of mankind?

"Anyway, it might be for the best that we can't meet up," said Milo.

"Why?" I said.

"Well, I have an idea for how we get around your singing … uh … deficiency."

I perked up a little. "You do? How?"

Milo tapped his nose. "Leave it with me. Let's just say I'm working on something, but it's going to take me some time."

I didn't like being kept in the dark over something as important as this, but I trusted Milo. I knew he wouldn't let me down. "Must be nice to have talents," I said.

"If this works, you won't need to be talented," said Milo. "At least not in the singing department. How are you getting on with that other thing?"

"You mean the dancing?" I said. "Terribly."

"Oh," said Milo. "Well, keep at it. I'm sure you'll get the hang of it soon."

Milo may have been the smartest kid I knew, but he wasn't a very good liar, and I could hear it in his voice that he didn't believe what he was saying.

"Oh, before I go, one more thing," he added. "The last piece of the boy band puzzle. You need to get a haircut. A cool haircut."

I looked at the picture of myself in the corner of the screen. My hair was what my mom called "mousy brown." It was a little long now and I had bangs that seemed to do whatever they liked. I guess I could do with a trim. Or maybe even just a comb. But overall I didn't see anything too bad about it.

"What's wrong with this one?" I asked.

"Nothing," he said. "If you're trying to join a boy band from twenty years ago. Are you?"

"No," I said.

"Then you need something up-to-date. Something with sharp edges and weird angles and whooshes."

"Right," I said, wondering how I'd explain all this to Mr. Johnstone, the grumpy eighty-six-year-old man who normally cuts my hair. "Well, I better get back to practicing my dancing."

We ended the call. But instead of getting up, I put my head on the desk.

The entire world is at stake, said a voice in my head.

The voice was annoying.

It was also right.

I took Milo's instructions out of my pocket and placed them on my bed. I selected an upbeat track on the media player. I nodded my head in time to the beat. And then I began.

SMASH!

Ah well, I never liked that mug anyway.

An hour later, I was panting and sweaty, but I still hadn't mastered that routine. All I had done was stomp aimlessly around my room like a blind and angry octopus, knocking things over as I went. If that's what Apocalips were looking for in their next member then we'd all be in luck.

I had just clicked "play" again when there was a knock on my door. I stopped the track and opened it. Mom and Dad were standing there.

"What?" I said. "Come to remind me how useless I am?"

They both looked at me with hurt expressions, and I immediately regretted saying it.

"I'm sorry," I said. "If it's about the noise, I'll try and keep it down."

Mom shook her head. "No, it's not that," she said. "Look, Sam, do you really want to go through with this?"

"I have to," I said.

Mom looked at Dad, who nodded. "All right," he said. "Then we want to help."

I laughed. "No offense," I said. "But how could you two possibly help?"

"It's time we told you the story of how we first met," said Dad.

I rolled my eyes. "You've already told me that a hundred times," I said. "You met when you were studying to be accountants."

Mom was staring at the ground. "No," she said quietly. "The *real* story of how we met."

APOCALIPS

CHAPTER NINE

★ ★ ★

"We weren't always accountants," said Dad in a somber voice as the three of us sat down at the kitchen table.

"And we met before we became accountants," said Mom, fiddling with her necklace. "Long before."

"The year was 1997," said Dad. "It was a time of Spice Girls and Tamagotchis."

"What?" I asked.

"They were these little toy pets that you had to feed and toilet train," said Mom.

I nodded. "OK. And what were Tamagotchis?"

"No, son, I…" said Dad, "Oh, look, it doesn't matter. The important thing is that it was the year that your mom and I met at the audition."

"Audition?" I repeated.

"We were both young and ambitious," said Mom. "We wanted to be singers. We wanted to be stars. So we both answered a call for members of a new pop group."

I looked around for the hidden cameras I was sure were watching me.

"It was supposed to be a group of five," said Mom. "Three girls and two boys. But the chemistry between your father and me was incredible."

I squirmed a little at the word "chemistry."

"It was love at first sight," said Dad as he took Mom's hand and stared longingly into her eyes.

I squirmed even more at that.

"We knew straightaway that we were meant for each other," said Mom, nuzzling her nose into Dad's.

"All right, that's plenty," I said. "Can we get back to the story?"

Dad smiled. "Well, after seeing your mom and me perform together, the man auditioning us decided to go with a two-piece instead."

"He named us **2-Incredible**," said Mom, staring wistfully into the distance.

The name triggered something in my memory. "2-Incredible," I said. "I know that name from somewhere…"

"Don't Be Stupid," said Dad.

"There's no need to be like that," I said, folding my arms. "I just thought I recognized the name."

"No," laughed Dad. "That was the name of our song. 'Don't Be Stupid.'"

"Oh," I said. "Wait, I know that song. Everyone does. They still play it all the time."

"It went straight to number one," said Dad, looking proud. "Stayed there for four weeks."

"We were an overnight success," said Mom. "Suddenly we were everywhere. Our faces were all over the TV and magazines. I even saw us on the side of a bus once. Imagine! A bus."

"We were invited to all the best parties. Award ceremonies and film premieres, you name it," continued Dad. "And the gossip columns in the newspapers loved us. They tracked our relationship in minute detail."

"They knew things about us that we didn't even know," said Mom. "Of course most of it was made up.

We never did go snowboarding with Oasis and I have no idea where us getting drunk in a hot-air balloon with Kylie came from."

"And that was the problem, son," said Dad. "It became too much for us. It's a lot of pressure to have everything you do reported to the entire country. It was a very stressful time. Your mom and I began to argue. A lot."

"Eventually we realized that the only way our relationship was going to work was if we gave up the music," said Mom. "So that's what we did."

I was finding pretty much everything they were saying hard to take in, but this was almost impossible to imagine. They could have had it all – fame, money, success, a pool in their backyard shaped like a palm tree. "You just walked away?" I said.

They nodded. "It was the hardest decision of our lives," said Dad. "Our manager hit the roof. He threatened to sue. Said he was going to destroy us."

"So what happened?" I asked.

"'Stop Asking Silly Questions,'" said Mom.

"But I just wanted to know…" I said.

"No," said Mom. "'Stop Asking Silly Questions' was the name of our second single. Before we got the chance to publicly announce that 2-Incredible were no more, our manager went ahead and released it. But it only got to number two in the charts, so he called us to say we were old news and that he was dropping us. We decided not to point out that we had already quit."

I realized something had been bugging me about this whole story. "Hang on a second," I said. "I've seen pictures of 2-Incredible, and they look nothing like you."

Dad stood up and switched on the kettle.

"You don't just walk away from being as famous as we were," he said, taking two mugs out of the cupboard. "Not easily anyway."

"We went into hiding," said Mom. "We changed everything we could. Our address, our appearances, even our names. The world knew us as Cat and D—"

"D?" I interrupted, looking at my dad.

"Oh yeah, back then one-letter names were all the rage," he said. "J, H, one guy even changed his to P. So Dave became D."

"When we quit, we started going by our middle names and became boring old Harold and Martha instead."

"I grew this beard and put on thirty pounds," said Dad.

Mom frowned. "Again, I'm not sure either of those was actually necessary, dear."

"Then we went back to college and became accountants," sighed Dad. "And that was that."

A silence fell over the kitchen. Mom stared at the floor as Dad looked out of the window. I was stunned by their story. How could any of this be true? How could my award-winningly dull parents actually be former pop sensations? It was like trying to imagine the Heatherstones saying something nice to me.

But the more I watched them, the more I felt

sorry for them. I could tell there was regret there.
A lot of it.

"Do you miss it?" I asked them. "Being famous,
I mean?"

Mom and Dad looked at each other. Then the
kettle boiled.

"Yes and no," said Mom as Dad made the
tea. "We don't regret the decision we made. We
might never have had you and Lexi otherwise.
And we definitely don't miss every little thing we
did showing up in the papers the following day.
Reporters going through our trash and hacking our
phones, or getting in our faces with their cameras
the moment we stepped out of the house.

"But we miss the other side," Mom continued.
"The performing. That's what your dad and I really
loved. That all ended a bit too quickly."

I nodded as if I understood, though I doubted
I ever could.

Dad joined us at the table, putting down two
cups of tea on the table. I got up and fetched a can

of cola from the fridge.

"Sorry we've kept it from you," he said. "We were planning on telling you both one day, but it's not the sort of thing you just announce over breakfast, is it? Morning, everyone, yes, I will have some toast. Oh, that reminds me – your mother and I used to be massive pop stars. Pass the butter, will you?"

"Now seemed like as good a time as any," said Mom. "How about it, Sam? Maybe we can finally put our skills to use again."

We sat in silence for a bit. It was a lot to take in. I cracked open the can and finished the entire thing in a couple of gulps.

"You really think you can help me?" I asked, letting out a loud belch.

Dad took a sip of tea. "As much as anyone can in four days," he said.

"But you understand that we can't help with your singing?" said Mom. "I say this with love, sweetheart – honestly, I don't think all the time in the world could help you there. And that's quite important for a pop star."

I let Mom's comments slide, mostly on account of them being perfectly correct.

"Let me worry about that," I said, which obviously I was. "I just need to learn how to dance."

"That we can teach you," said Dad.

"Brilliant!" I said, putting the paper with Milo's routine on it in my pocket. "Though it's going to get a bit cramped in my room…"

"We won't be needing your room," said Mom. "We'll be using the studio."

I looked at them blankly. "What studio?"

Mom and Dad exchanged confused glances.

"Oh, right," said Dad as if something had dawned on him. "We haven't told you about that either, have we?"

APOCALIPS

CHAPTER TEN

★★★

Our house is the only house I've ever lived in. There's nothing very interesting about it. It looks like every other one on our street. It has four bedrooms, a living room, a dining room, a kitchen, a bathroom and an attic. Oh, and a cellar, but I've never been down there as my parents had to seal it off because of safety concerns.

Well, that's what they told me.

"Surprise," said Mom, waving her hands around theatrically in a not-very-subtle attempt to sidestep the fact that she and my dad had managed to keep a lie this big from me my whole life.

"Mom … Dad," I said. "Why is there a dance studio in our cellar?"

When I say dance studio, I don't just mean it was an average basement with a space cleared in the middle in case someone wanted to bust a move from time to time. The room was huge. It was longer than our house, which meant that most of it had to be directly under our front yard and backyard. The polished wooden floor creaked a little as I walked over it, and I could see my own astonishment in the mirror that ran along the entire length of one of the walls.

"We knew most of it had to come to an end," said Dad, "but the dancing didn't have to."

"After getting the house," continued Mom, "we still had a bit of money left over from our record sales. So we spent it on this. Our secret hideaway."

"You've heard of man caves," said Dad. "This is our dance cave."

"We come down here sometimes when you and Lexi are asleep," said Mom.

"So those times I heard banging in the middle of the night and you told me it was probably just really big rats…" I said.

"Yeah, that would have been us," said Dad. "Anyway, enough talking. Let's get started. So what do you want to learn first?"

I scratched my head. The only dances I even knew the name of were the waltz, the tango and the hokey pokey, and I knew they weren't going to cut it. I took Milo's dance routine from my back pocket. "I've been trying to learn this one," I said. "But I just can't get it."

Dad unfolded the paper.

"Well, I'm not surprised," he said. "This is the Florentine Fandango. It's way too hard for a beginner. Most professionals wouldn't even attempt it without having a paramedic on standby."

"Well, do you know any dances that I *would* be able to learn in the next few days?" I asked, trying not to think about the time I'd already wasted.

"Oh, tons," said Dad. "Off the top of my head there's the Charleston. The rumba. The Swamp Monster. The Flying Knuckle. The Hungry Hippo. The Mad Doctor. The Pot-Bellied Sailor. Sammo's Pit Stop. The Rocking Robber. The Silent Pensioner. The Haunted Futon. The Cranky Dragon. The Sad Potato. The Masked Train Conductor. The Irritating Chess Master. The Weeping Milk Bottle. The Crafty Beagle. The Bored Pumpkin. The Ace of Suedes. The Dance of a Thousand Frogs. The Whispering Kettle. The Tunneling Badger. The Honky-Tonk Parking Attendant. The Lazy Bongo. The Shy Raccoon. The Cheesy Weasel. The Sinister Chihuahua.

The Hovering Postman. The Nasty Chicken. The Winter of Discontent. The Rolling Pigeon. The Snarling Grandpa. The Fidgety Wolf. The Tickling Princess. The Half-Baked Yo-Yo. The Forgetful Caterpillar. The Blue Monkey Shuffle."

I blinked a few times. "You really know all those?"

Dad nodded. "Sure. And there's more. The Barnyard Breakdance. The Mad Meteor. The Reluctant Rodeo Clown. The Family of Traveling Mosquitoes. The—"

"All right, honey, that's plenty," said Mom. "Let's start with something simple, and we can build up to a few of those other ones."

The next few days passed in a blur. Mom and Dad were perfectionists. I spent hours drilling the same moves over and over again. But eventually something odd started to happen. I got better. A lot better.

By Wednesday I could do the Midtown Manhattan Traffic Jam.

By Thursday I had the Big Dipper Blowout mastered.

And on Friday I finally cracked the Jittery Panda.

"And if that doesn't work, you've always got the Difficult Mother-In-Law or the Brittle Box-Car Boogie to fall back on," said Dad.

"Right," I said. "Thanks, guys. I think I'm ready for tomorrow."

Well, that wasn't quite true. I hadn't heard from Milo in days. The Apocalytes were still patrolling the streets, and he wasn't returning my calls or emails. I could only hope that his big idea to improve my singing would materialize. My dancing was a lot better than it was at the start of the week, but there wasn't a dance in the world that could cover for my horrible voice.

And then there was that other thing that Milo had talked about. The third key component of being a successful boy band member. That's why Mom had just appeared at the studio door with some clippers and a bunch of her hair products.

"Ready, Sam?" she said. "Let's take this upstairs. I don't want hair all over the dance floor."

An hour later, I sat on a stool in the kitchen, unable to recognize the boy looking back at me in Mom's hand mirror. Gone was the plain, unexciting arrangement of hair that normally kept my head warm like a sensible, functional furry hat. In its place was a brash, cocky mane, all straight lines and strange angles, a mash-up of whooshes, attitude and gel. Thanks to some strange-smelling liquids that Mom assured me were fine, my hair was also now at least eighty percent blonder than before. It was in your face and in my face and it didn't care. It was a boy band haircut.

I was turning my head to get a different view when another face appeared in the mirror, almost causing me to fall off the stool.

"Lexi!" said Mom. "What do you think of your brother's new 'do? Doesn't he look handsome?"

I had barely seen my sister the whole week. I had been in training most of the time, and Lexi had spent her days with Amy and the Heatherstones. She still had on the same black dress that all the Apocalytes were wearing.

"Looks ridiculous," she said. "What's that for?"

"Your brother's audition tomorrow, of course," said Mom. "You remember, I told you?"

Lexi flinched a little, a look of confusion filling her face. "I thought you were joking," she said.

"Oh no," said Mom. "Your brother's going to be the next Justin Bieber. Well, he's going to give it a try anyway."

"Martha," shouted Dad from the living room. "Have you seen those tax legislation notes I need for the Harwick account?"

"They're in the red binder," Mom shouted back. "Hang on, I'll show you."

Mom headed toward the door before pausing. She looked at me and sighed. "It was nice to be in a world that didn't involve accountancy for once. Back to reality, I suppose."

When she had gone, Lexi turned to me. "You're … *you're* … actually going through with it?"

I nodded. "That's right," I said. "And I'm going to win. And when I do I promise I'm going to figure out what they've done to you."

"Done to me?" she scoffed. "What are you talking about, Sam? No one has done anything to me. I'm exactly the same as I always was. And *you* win? You … join Apocalips? The thought of … the thought of … you…"

Her voice drifted off, then for a brief moment the glassy look in her eyes faded, and I caught a glimpse of the real Lexi. "Sam … help…" she whispered.

"Lexi!" I shouted, grabbing her with both hands and looking her in the eyes, but as soon as I did that they hardened again, and I knew she was gone. Without uttering another word, Lexi shoved me aside and headed upstairs. Seconds later the sounds of "Baby, Baby, Baby, Baby" filled the house.

I thought about the promise I had made to get to the bottom of what Apocalips had done to her. Now perhaps I finally stood a chance. I had the look and I had the moves. Well, I had some moves, at least. But I was still missing a key ingredient – singing.

Where was Milo?

APOCALIPS

CHAPTER ELEVEN

★★★

After spending most of the night lying awake worrying about the audition, I had finally managed to drift off when Milo burst into my room.

"I've done it!" he shouted. "I've only gone and done it! Ouch!"

The ouch was because I'd instinctively thrown my pillow at his head. "Done what?" I moaned. "What time is it?"

"You know, your mom asked me the same thing when she opened the door for me," said Milo. "It's half-past six. And you should be up by now. The auditions are at nine."

"I know," I said. "I haven't had much sleep, no thanks to you. Where have you been?"

"Where do you think I've been?" said Milo defensively. "I've been holed up trying to solve our vocal problem. That's why I'm here. I've done it. I've figured out how you're going to win this competition."

Milo pulled open the curtains, allowing the early morning light to flood into the room where it proceeded to burn my eyes out of their sockets. I pulled the covers over my head.

"Does your plan involve blinding me?" I asked.

"No," said Milo. "It involves this."

I pulled the covers down a little but still had to squint to see what Milo was holding. In the light it almost looked like a...

"Is that a retainer?" I asked.

Milo looked affronted. "This is the key to saving the world."

"Yes, but is it a retainer?"

"This is my state-of-the-art patent-pending

invention that allows sound to be wirelessly transmitted from one location to another. It's a Wi-Fi-enabled mouth speaker. I call it the Sing-Sync."

I nodded. "It's a retainer though, isn't it?"

Milo looked exasperated. "No, it's... Yes, all right, fine, it's a retainer. Will you just try it?"

I took the retainer and inserted it into my mouth. A horrible thought occurred to me. "Wait. Is this *your* retainer?"

Milo rolled his eyes. "I did wash it."

"EEEUUUUUURRRGGGGGHHHHHH!"

"Well, now you're just being rude," said Milo.

"That's disgusting," I said.

"Just wait," said Milo, grabbing my phone and tapping some buttons. An Apocalips song called "Fun with My Besties" began to play. Except the sound of Steve yeah-yeah-yeahing wasn't coming from the phone, it was coming from my mouth.

I couldn't believe it. "This is amazing."

Milo shrugged. "I know."

I began miming the words to the song as I danced around the room in my pajamas. "It's like I'm the one actually singing it," I said, once it had finished. "I mean, apart from the backing track."

"Don't worry," said Milo. "I'll have that fixed for the audition. Oh, and it transmits both ways so I'll be able to hear what's going on. We'd better use the manual settings, just in case there's a problem with the signal. And it doesn't have a lot of power, so only turn it on when you need it. There's a switch on the left-hand side."

"You mean I'll have to wear it the whole time?" I asked, managing to flick the switch with my tongue. "I'm not sure braces are the right look for a boy band member."

Milo looked put out. "First of all," he said, "it's not braces, it's a retainer. Big difference. Second of all, if you had any knowledge of current trends, you'd know they're actually a must-have fashion accessory these days. All the big celebrities have them now. Why do you think I had one?"

"Your crooked teeth?" I suggested.

Milo paused. "Well … yeah, partly because of that," he said. "But I was actually leaning toward getting one anyway. And I have to say it goes quite well with that new haircut of yours."

I smiled at myself in the mirror. To my surprise, Milo was right, it didn't look that bad. Thanks to the ten tons of hair product that Mom had slapped on my head, my hair looked exactly like it did the night before. My pillow, meanwhile, was ripped to shreds, thanks to all the sharp points and jagged edges.

"Talking of your image," said Milo. "Have you decided what you're going to wear today?"

"Oh," I said. Not only had I not decided, I hadn't even thought about it. "I dunno. Maybe a shirt and tie? Some trousers?"

"You're auditioning for a boy band not interviewing for a job at a bank," Milo replied. "What would you do without me?" He handed me a plastic bag. Inside was a T-shirt featuring some punk band from the seventies. Whoever they were, they seemed to like smashing guitars. There was also a pair of navy-blue jeans that were clearly too small for me. And then, for some reason, a dinner jacket.

"Perfect. It strikes just the right balance between safe and dangerous," Milo said, once I had put them on. "The thin line that all successful boy bands walk: familiar and comfortable, sure, but not without risk."

"A bit like a kettle?" I asked.

Milo sighed. "Yeah, if you like."

We went downstairs for breakfast where I was greeted with a round of applause from my parents.

"Look at you!" said Mom. "Harold, look at him."

"I am looking," said Dad. "Why have you got braces?"

"It's a retainer," I said. "And because it looks good. Apparently."

Dad didn't look too convinced but nodded anyway before returning to eat his toast.

While Milo had no problem tucking into a bowl

of Cheery-Loops, I would have preferred to skip breakfast. The nerves were sending clear signals to my stomach that food was not welcome. But Mom was having none of it. She sat me down at the table and practically force-fed me some toast.

"No one ever got into a boy band on an empty stomach," she told me.

"How could you possibly know that?" I asked. "Have you done the research?"

"And no one ever got into a boy band with a smart mouth," she added. Well, I was pretty sure that one wasn't true.

As I finished my toast and washed it down with some orange juice, Dad stood up from the table. "Right then," he said, checking his watch. "Are we all ready?"

"There's just one more thing I have to do," I said, clutching my stomach.

After a very long trip to the bathroom, we set off in the car. My parents up front and Milo, because he was the smallest, sitting in the middle of the back seat between me and Lexi. She wanted to be there with the rest of the Apocalytes to see the new member unveiled. She hadn't spoken a word to me since the previous day. In fact, she had barely even looked at me.

"Is your sister still ... you know?" whispered Milo.

"Yeah," I hissed. "Though there was something yesterday. When she found out I was going to the audition there was a moment where she came back... But then she was gone again."

Milo's brow furrowed a little. "Interesting..."

"Thanks for coming with me," I said, knowing it would be difficult for Milo given how many people were likely to be there.

"No bother," said Milo, even though the look on his face said the opposite was true. "Besides, the range of the device isn't that great. The closer I am to you, the better things should go."

Eventually the car lurched to a stop, and my heart fell through the floor. I mean, it didn't literally fall through the floor. Because if that had happened I wouldn't have to go through with the audition, and I definitely wasn't that lucky.

We had arrived.

"Oh. Whoa," I said.

There had to be tens of thousands of hopefuls gathered outside the arena. My exciting new look suddenly didn't seem so exciting. Here it just looked normal. Boring even.

"It's like Night of the Walking Hipsters," said Milo as we walked toward the gate. We were met by a burly-looking man carrying a notepad in one hand and a pen in the other. Underneath his right arm was a huge roll of purple stickers. He looked almost as happy to be there as I was.

"Name?" he barked.

"Um… Sam Miller. I'm here for the audition?"

The man looked at me with a deadpan expression. "No? Really? I never would have guessed. I thought you might have come to see me. Oh well, I guess ol' Brian will just have to do without your scintillating company on this fine day."

"You're a very sarcastic man, Brian," said Mom, giving him a stern look.

"Yeah, well, you would be too if you'd had to put up with the number of fame-hungry brats I've had to this morning," said Brian. He looked at Mom with suspicion. "I hope you weren't planning on entering, madam? It's boys only, I'm afraid. My boss was very specific about that."

"Of course I'm not," snapped Mom.

"You'd be surprised," said Brian. "You wouldn't be the first non-boy we've had to turn away this morning. We've had young girls, old ladies, middle-aged men. Someone even tried to enter their dog. Actually, it was a shame we had to turn that one away, to be honest. He was a lot better than most of the fame-hungry wannabes, let me tell you. Anyway, if you're not applying, you'll need to move on."

"Can't we come in to lend him support?" asked Milo.

"Nope. Auditionees only, I'm afraid. Friends and family can gather around the other side of the building. That's where the unveiling of the winner will take place."

"How long will that be?" asked Dad.

"Oh, at least eight hours or so, I'd imagine," said Brian, slapping a purple sticker on my chest that said "**ENTRANT 4593**." He looked me up and down then added: "Although if you're just waiting for this one, I'm sure you won't be waiting long."

"Thanks a lot," I said.

"Don't listen to him," said Milo. "You've got this. Or rather, we've got this. And remember what I said about the Sing-Sync."

I had to think for a second what he was talking about. "Oh, you mean the retainer?"

Milo sighed. "It's not a… Look, we don't have time for this argument again. Like I said before, there's not a lot of juice in the battery, so only switch it on when you need it. Got it?"

"Got it."

"All right, then. Well, this is it," he said, slapping me on the shoulder before leaning in and whispering, "Good luck. Remember, the fate of the entire world depends on you."

"So no pressure then," I said, grinning.

But Milo wasn't smiling. "No, quite the opposite," he said. "There's more pressure on you than perhaps anyone in history."

"Your pep talks are terrible," I said.

I said my last goodbyes and pried myself free from Mom's arms. I looked for Lexi, but she had already hurried around to the front with the other Apocalytes. As I made my way through the gate into the mass of wannabes, I looked around at all the bright, hopeful faces. For me, though, it wasn't about becoming famous. I was here to save the world, and the only way to do that would be to crush the dreams of every single one of them.

APOCALIPS

CHAPTER TWELVE

★★★

Dreams were not the only thing likely to be crushed that day. Inside the arena, thousands of hopefuls were squashed up against each other, crammed inside a penned-off area that took up about half the space.

"It's like being in a can of sardines," said someone.

"It's nowhere near as roomy as that," said someone else.

On the plus side, the discomfort was helping keep my mind off what was to come. I was far too preoccupied with trying to minimize the pain being caused by the shoulder in my face and the elbow in my ribs to worry about the audition and/or the fate of the world. The shoulder in question belonged to a tanned boy with long blond hair who looked like he had just stepped off the set of an Australian soap opera. The elbow meanwhile was attached to a smaller boy, decked out in a leather jacket and sunglasses. To me he seemed more like someone auditioning for the role of an action-movie star from the eighties than a boy band. He did not look particularly pleased.

The surfer boy nodded at me. "'Sup?" he said.

"Oh… Yeah … 'Sup," I said, trying and failing to act cool.

"Name's Mickey," he said. "People call me Mickey."

"That makes sense, I guess," I said. "I'm Sam."

"Saaaaam," repeated Mickey as if his mouth was trying the word out for size. "Cool. Like it. Sam. Sam the man. Sam you am. So, Sam, you hyped for this or what? I'm off the wall. Well, I would be if there weren't all these people in the way."

I nodded. "Yep. Excited."

"It's going to be amaaaazing. You been at this long, Sam you am?"

I checked my watch. "About an hour or so."

Mickey laughed. "No, man, not this. I mean *this.*" His eyes scanned the crowd in a manner that suggested he was explaining what he meant, but I still didn't get what he was talking about. Before I could ask him, I heard a long, drawn-out sigh to my right.

"He means, how long have you been on the circuit?" said the annoyed-looking boy, now looking even more annoyed.

"Oh, right," I said. "About an hour or so."

Annoyed Boy put no effort whatsoever into stifling a laugh.

"Hey, dude, be cool," Mickey told him. "Everyone's got to start somewhere. And as my mom always says, it doesn't matter how many nos you get, you only need one yes."

Annoyed Boy said nothing, but I caught him rolling his eyes. I turned back toward Mickey. "How many auditions have you been to?" I asked.

"Me? Ah man, tons. I've lost count, actually. Tried out for a bunch of bands. Some acting, too. And modeling. Commercials. You name it really. Got one gig doing a voice for a skateboarding cat. That was pretty sweet."

I could hear more sniggering to my left.

"Something funny, bud?" asked Mickey.

Annoyed Boy stopped laughing and looked at us both with disgust. "As a matter of fact, yes. I was laughing because I had been foolish enough to think that I might face some actual competition today.

But if a first-timer and a skateboarding cat are the best on offer, then it's going to be a very short audition."

"I wasn't actually a cat," said Mickey. "I was the voice of a cat."

"Yes, thanks for clearing that up," said Annoyed Boy.

"Ignore him," I told Mickey. "He's just trying to wind you up." Part of me realized that it might be better to let Mickey stay riled. He seemed like a nice guy, but I had to win this competition. If Mickey was thrown off his game a little, then that was good for me.

Even so, the idea didn't sit well with me, despite the fact that I knew I was going to have to cheat to win this thing. The longer I could keep my hands clean, the better.

Mickey looked like he was about to reply to Annoyed Boy when the lights went out. A spotlight appeared onstage, shining on three people who were sitting behind a large desk.

"Greetings," boomed a voice over the loudspeakers. On the giant screens above was a familiar-looking face. With his bronze skin and jet-black hair he resembled an orange dipped in tar. He wore a signature blue silk shirt with one too many buttons undone and a pair of completely unnecessary sunglasses. I remembered seeing a newspaper front page recently where he was celebrating his 40th birthday, but thanks to the vast amount of cosmetic surgery he'd had, he didn't look a day past fifty-eight.

"For those that don't know me, as unlikely as that may be, my name is Nigel Cruul. You should be familiar with me from shows like Pop Star Rodeo, Pop Star Charades, Stop! That's My Pop Star, Pop Star with a Vengeance, I Can't Believe That's a Pop Star, The Top 1000 Pop Stars Born in October and, of course, the legendary Pop Stars Eating Weird Things. Beloved classics, each and every one. But I am here today not in my capacity as a celebrated star of loosely music-based quality prime-time television shows but instead in my main role as the manager of the greatest pop band of all time – Apocalips."

The arena went wild at the mention of the band's name.

"Unfortunately the band won't be joining us today," continued Cruul, "as they're incredibly busy rehearsing. And also, to be honest, they just didn't want to." The cheers of the crowd fizzled out quite quickly after that.

I was well aware of Nigel Cruul. Everyone was.

It made no difference if you had never actually seen any of his shows. He was one of those celebrities where no matter how little interest you have in them, you still end up knowing more about them than your own friends. Cruul was famously mean and seemed to take great pleasure in handing out insults. In fact, he seemed to enjoy doing that far more than he appeared to enjoy finding people with actual talent.

"We're going to have a lot of fun today," said Cruul, a sinister smile creeping across his wrinkle- and blemish-free face. "Among you hopefuls is the next member of Apocalips. My job today, and the job of this panel, is to find that person. Forget what you know about the audition process – it will not help you here. No amount of preparation can prepare you for what we will put you through today. Our methods may not be fair, they may not be nice, they may not even appear to make any sense, but they are most certainly methods. Now, allow me to introduce the people who will be helping me today. First of all, we have a veteran voice in the form of the amazing Annabelle."

The image on the screen switched to that of Annabelle Santos, one of the most successful music artists of all time. As Cruul said, she was exceptionally talented but had a fierce reputation for being ruthless, vindictive and obsessed with maintaining her status. She had been around for what felt like forever, which was odd because she was actually only ten years old. She was the oldest little girl the world had ever seen, constantly changing her image – today she was sporting rainbow-colored hair and a red catsuit with massive spikes on her shoulders.

"I've been in this industry a long time," she said, in between long gulps of coffee. "Nothing takes me by surprise or catches me off guard. But that's exactly what I expect from anyone who wants to make the band. I don't just want the exceptional, I want the impossible."

"Wise words there," said Cruul. "Our other judge needs no introduction. But for some reason he insists on it anyway. It's Dominic Douglas."

I knew three things about Dominic Douglas:

1. He was a music producer who specialized in boy bands, launching some of the most successful groups in history including All About the Boys, Boyz City and The Boy-Street Boys.

2. He was once voted the World's Most Boring Man.

3. He had a long-standing feud with Nigel Cruul, but for some reason they still ended up doing tons of TV shows together.

"Hello, everyone," said Douglas, in a light Scottish accent. "Good luck to you all. Remember that if you want to win this thing you're going to have to give one hundred percent."

"It's going to take more than that," said Cruul, in a snippy tone. "A thousand percent is more like it."

Douglas gave Cruul a confused look. "They'll hardly be able to do that," he said. "One hundred percent is the maximum anyone can give. The only way to give a thousand percent would be to clone another nine versions of themselves, each performing at one hundred percent. That's just math, Nigel."

"We said we expected the impossible," said Cruul.

"If you cloned nineteen versions of yourself they'd each only have to perform at fifty percent," offered Annabelle.

"Yes, that's right," agreed Dominic. "You could give one thousand percent quite comfortably given access to cloning technology. Although I think for now we should have a blanket ban on the use of clones, given that there is barely enough room in here as it is, let alone ten or twenty times as many. We have fire regulations to consider."

Cruul was holding his head in his hands as if he had a migraine. "Will you please be quiet? Although you do have a point. There are an awful lot of people here. Luckily we have ways of quickly thinning out the contenders from the pretenders. So let's get things started."

I could feel a buzz start to spread through the crowd. The screens above showed security guards removing the ropes that surrounded us, releasing us from our pen.

"OK, nice and simple," said Cruul. "Everyone who currently has a girlfriend, move to the left-hand side of the arena. Everyone else move to the right."

I looked at Mickey and was at least partially relieved to see that he seemed just as confused as I was. In fact, almost everywhere I looked I saw the same bewildered expressions. Except one. Annoyed Boy. He had the most irritating smirk on his face.

"Come on," said Cruul. "This isn't difficult, people. Left if you're a Romeo, right if you're not."

"See you later, losers," said Annoyed Boy as he began to head left.

Mickey looked unconvinced. "No way do you have a girlfriend," he said.

"And who's going to prove it?" asked Annoyed Boy. "You heard him. *Romeos.* They want someone who appeals to girls, not dateless wonders like the two of you. Don't worry, though, I'll be sure to look out for you both in the crowd when they unveil me as the winner."

I started to panic. Not only did I not have a girlfriend, I had never had one. The girls I knew were only ever interested in me for my ability to be easily tormented and shoved into storerooms. I was sure that wasn't what the judges would be looking for. Maybe Annoyed Boy had the right idea. No one would know if I didn't have a girlfriend. Well, no one here, anyway. And I wouldn't even need to flat-out lie. All I'd really be doing was walking left instead of right.

I took a single step to my left, but before I could take another one, I felt a hand grasp me by the shoulder. I looked up at Mickey.

"Don't do it, Sam," he said. "Trust me."

I wasn't sure what to do. The fate of the world literally depended on me making the right move. Left or right. Mickey began walking right. I sighed and followed him, taking my place with the rest of the dateless wonders.

After a few minutes, when the left and right camps

had been formed, Nigel Cruul spoke again. "Good. Now, one of the most important skills required to be in a boy band is the ability to follow orders. So, well done to you all for that. Unfortunately, another important aspect of being in a boy band is the appearance of availability to your fans. In other words: no girlfriends. Those on the left, thank you for coming, your services are no longer required. Please vacate the premises immediately."

The arena erupted in a mix of outrage and delight. Needless to say, I was in the happier of the two camps. On the big screens above they were showing Annoyed Boy, or to put it more accurately, Meltdown Boy, refusing to budge and being picked up by an enormous security guard and carried toward the doors. At least he'd gotten one thing correct – his audition hadn't taken very long.

I breathed a sigh of relief that I had made it past the first hurdle. I mouthed the words "Thank you" at Mickey, who smiled and nodded. Even though I knew it couldn't last, for now at least, I had an ally.

APOCALiPS

CHAPTER THIRTEEN

★ ★ ★

Whether they had been telling the truth or not, many had followed the same fate of Annoyed Boy. I guessed that at least half of those auditioning had been eliminated. Which still left plenty of nervous boy band wannabes waiting to find out their fate. Most wouldn't have to wait long.

"Congratulations to those of you still with us," said Nigel Cruul, taking his place with the rest of the judges at the table. "But unfortunately, from here on in, it only gets more difficult. So let's begin. There will be three tests – each one of us judges has come up with a different challenge. The first one is mine, and it's designed to get a feel for your personality."

"Uh-oh," said Mickey.

"Personality is crucial to a boy band member," continued Cruul as security staff moved quickly through the hall, reshaping us all into one long, winding line. "And not just in appealing to your fans. Remember that if you win you're going to be on the road 24/7, sometimes 25/8, for months on end with a group of guys who are as close-knit as you can get. It's vital that whoever joins Apocalips is the type of person who can come in and instantly gel with the incredible group dynamic they have. To assess this, each of you will come onstage in turn, and we will judge you on your personality. Please note, singing will not be required at this stage."

A murmur went through the crowd at this. No singing? At a contest to be the lead singer in a boy band?

Mickey was shaking his head.

"What is it?" I asked.

"I've seen this before," he said. "Believe me, they're not interested in anyone's personality."

"What do you mean?"

"You'll see soon enough," said Mickey, pointing toward the stage where the first of the auditionees was stepping into the spotlight. I could hear some of the boys around us sniggering as they looked up at the screens, but I couldn't tell what was funny.

"What are they laughing at?" I asked.

For the first time since I'd met him, Mickey suddenly didn't look calm and composed anymore. He looked uneasy and slightly embarrassed. "His face," he said. "They're laughing at his face."

I still wasn't sure what I was supposed to be looking at. I glanced up at one of the big screens for a better look. As I took in the boy's magnified face I could see that he had some pimples ... all right, a lot of pimples. But that could hardly be a good enough reason to—

"Next," said Nigel Cruul. The boy's mouth dropped open and hung there for a few seconds.

"I said *next*," said Cruul. "Audition's over."

A mean-looking security guard was onstage in a flash, dragging off the poor kid.

"They didn't even ask him a question," I said.

"Of course not," said Mickey.

"But how can they learn anything about someone's personality if they don't even bother speaking to them?"

"They don't," said Mickey. "Because that's not what this is about. They're not interested in people's personalities – they're interested in whether your face fits. It's like when I go for a modeling job, and someone looks me up and down, and makes a judgement just like that. That's all this is – except in front of an audience."

"But surely it's about more than looks?" I said. "Doesn't this seem kind of cruel?"

"Hey, you don't need to tell me," said Mickey, "but to these guys, image is everything."

I watched in horror as boy after boy took to the stage only to be sent packing with barely so much as a glance from the judges. Every now and again they'd actually send someone through, but I couldn't for the life of me tell what they had that the others didn't. Almost without realizing, I started fiddling with the ends of my hair, checking that they were still suitably pointy. Would I even get a chance?

It bothered me more than I wanted to admit and not just because of the whole needing to save the world thing. Obviously that was a pretty big deal, but it was more than that. For some reason it mattered to me to have the approval of those jerks. It was a horrible feeling.

"Say what you want about it," said Mickey, "but they're getting through the crowd. At this rate, we'll be done by lunchtime."

He was right. It wasn't pretty, but it was fast. For every boy who displayed the right amount of "personality," there were about thirty that didn't. The line moved forward at an alarming speed.

"You ready, Sam the man?" asked Mickey.

"No," I said meekly.

"Don't sweat it," he said, putting one of his huge arms around my shoulders. "The worst they can do is say no."

But Mickey was dead wrong on two counts. He couldn't begin to understand the consequences of what would happen if I failed. And that wasn't the worst they could do at all. The worst they could do was what they did to the boy right in front of me.

The boy was tall, even taller than Mickey. He was well dressed and well-groomed, and from the way he strutted onto the stage he had a natural confidence about him that I knew I'd never be able to replicate. I don't know what you call it, charisma maybe, but there was something instantly captivating about him, like he had been a star his whole life. He also happened to be…

"**FAT!**" blurted out Annabelle.

…slightly overweight.

In an instant the boy's confidence and swagger vanished, leaving a nervous and vulnerable-looking boy standing alone on the stage.

"I … I'm a really good singer," stammered the boy.

"Well, you're bound to be," said Cruul. "From all the suppers you've been singing for."

This sparked even more hilarity from the judges. Pockets of the crowd began to join them, too. It reminded me of the way some kids would laugh whenever the Heatherstones picked on me at school, in the hope that they would avoid having the same thing done to them. It never worked with the Heatherstones, and I doubted it was going to work with these bullies, either.

"In all my many, many years in this business," said ten-year-old Annabelle, "I've never see anyone as out of shape as you."

"Being in a boy band is a very physical career," said Dominic Douglas. "The average boy band member spends a third of his life jumping in the air, you know. I can't imagine you making it very far off the ground. It's not all sitting on stools, you know."

"And in his case they'd have to be reinforced stools," sniped Cruul. "Next!"

The boy's face turned bright red, and I could see his eyes starting to well up. He was frozen to the spot, unable to move. I couldn't stand by and watch any more, I knew I had to do something. Before I had even thought about what that might be, I was already marching across the stage.

"**ENOUGH!**" I shouted.

APOCALIPS

CHAPTER FOURTEEN

★ ★ ★

"Hold it right there," said Nigel Cruul, rising to his feet. Suddenly it was like someone had turned the light on, and I realized where I was and what I was doing. What *was* I doing? What was I *thinking*? Did I think storming the stage and demanding the judges apologize to the boy was somehow going to help the situation? You didn't have to be a seasoned audition-goer like Mickey to know that if this idea belonged anywhere it was at the top of a list called "Wrong things to do at an audition." And especially an audition where mankind's survival depended on you winning.

All eyes were on me now. On the plus side none of the judges seemed to be interested in abusing the boy anymore. He had finally managed to get his feet working and had wisely taken the opportunity to get himself off the stage, leaving me alone to face the firing squad.

"Wow," said Dominic, shaking his head in disbelief. "Just wow."

"Never in all my years in this business…" muttered Annabelle.

Nigel Cruul got up from behind the desk and began to make his way across the stage to me, with all the pace of a snail taking its time. His eyes were locked on mine, never once looking away or even blinking. He had a curious look on his face, which was a lot different from his normal looks of disgust, boredom and anger. Somehow, though, that didn't make him any less intimidating.

"What's your name?" he asked.

The question caught me off guard, mainly because it was the first one Cruul had asked anyone that day.

My mind decided to go completely blank. I knew the answer began with an *S*… Shane… Sean… Seamus? Actually, did it even begin with an *S*?

"Sam!" I finally blurted out.

"Sam, Sam, Sam," said Cruul, batting the word around like a cat toying with a mouse. "I want you to answer me one question."

"OK…" I said, trying to prepare myself for who knows what.

"I want you to tell me…"

"Who did your hair?" shouted Annabelle.

Cruul turned and scowled at her. "Yes … what she said."

"It's Michael St. Vincent, isn't it?" said Annabelle,

giving Dominic a knowing smile. "It's the straight edges and crazy angles that give it away."

Dominic wasn't having it. "That's clearly a Dorian De Winterbottom cut if ever I saw one."

"You're both idiots," snapped Cruul. "It's obviously the work of Penelope Hammerstein. She's a pioneer in swooshy haircuts. Well, put us out of our misery, Sam. Who cut your hair?"

"My … uh … mom," I said.

The judges exchanged confused looks. "Maya Mom?" said Dominic.

A look of realization dawned on the face of Annabelle. "Of course. Maya Mom. She's Russian … or American … or Chinese. She's from somewhere, anyway. I think I might have used her for the European leg of my Mushroom Teapot tour. Or was it the Snowflake Jungle tour? Oh, it was so long ago, I can't remember. But she's super reclusive. And super expensive. How on earth could you afford her? You don't look very rich to me, and I can usually tell. No disrespect."

"Er … none taken. She's my mother," I said, hoping to clear up the confusion.

"Your mother is Maya Mom?" asked Dominic. "Well, that's a stroke of luck."

"I've often said," began Cruul, adopting a thoughtful look, "that to make it in the business of show, one needs to have both talent and luck. Who you know can be very important."

"Oh, he's got a retainer, too," squealed Annabelle, clapping her tiny hands with glee. "Those are sooooo in right now. I'd get one, but unfortunately I'm cursed with perfect teeth."

"Sorry to hear that," I said.

"Thank you!" said Annabelle, putting her hands on her chest. "You're like the first person to ever say that."

"All right, enough," said Cruul. "Congratulations, Sam. You've made it through to the next round."

Before I could begin to process what had just happened, I found myself backstage with a couple of dozen other boys. For reasons none of them could get their heads around, they had all made it through. No one had sung a note. I had been the only contender who had even opened his mouth.

Moments later I let out a sigh of relief when Mickey walked through the curtain, joining us in the ranks of the confused but thankful.

"Sam the man," he said, slapping me playfully on the back with one of his huge hands. "We made it. That was a risky move you pulled back there…"

"The haircut?" I said. "I tried to tell them that it was my mom not— "

"I'm not talking about the haircut, man," he said. "I'm talking about you crashing the stage. You were actually going to defend that dude, weren't you?"

I looked at my feet, feeling shame wash over me that in the end, I hadn't. Obviously saving the world was more important, but it didn't stop me feeling bad for that boy. "Yeah, but I didn't…"

"That was still a pretty decent thing to do," he said. "You're a good guy, Sam. But I wouldn't worry too much. That kid'll be OK. I've seen him here and there – he really is a great singer. A voice like his, someone will be smart enough to give him a shot sooner or later."

"You think?"

Mickey nodded. "Talent can't be denied," he said. "That's what my mom says. Word to the wise, though. If I were you I wouldn't try anything like that again. You got lucky once, you probably won't be so lucky again. From here on in, it's all about talent."

APOCALiPS

CHAPTER FIFTEEN

★★★

That wasn't true. Not in the slightest.

In the end, thirty-two people made it through the curtain, out of thousands. It made sense that the singing part of the competition would now kick off. But nothing about this competition so far made sense.

We were herded back into the arena. Waiting for us, arranged in a single long line, were stools.

A boy standing next to us, sporting what could only be described as a floppy Mohawk, let out a long whistle. "Wow!" he said. "You know what those are, right?"

I took a guess. "Stools?"

"*Wooden* stools?" suggested Mickey.

The boy looked at us with genuine pity. "Stools? Well, yeah, obviously they're stools. But that's like saying the *Mona Lisa* is just a painting. They're much more than that. These are Fenecker's."

"Fenecker's?" asked Mickey, looking just as confused as I felt.

The boy looked exasperated. "Only the finest stool makers ever. Any boy band worth their salt uses Fenecker stools. You won't find a more comfortable or durable stool on earth."

"Right…" said Mickey. "Good stools. Got it."

A hush descended over the remaining contestants as Nigel, Annabelle and Dominic reappeared onstage.

"All right, the next challenge is…" said Cruul,

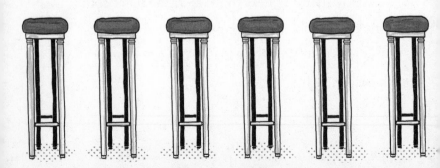

before letting out a long sigh, "Dominic's. As you can gather, it's got stools in it."

"Thank you, Nigel," said Dominic. "Now, being in a boy band requires tremendous coordination skills. It's a bit like being able to pat your head and rub your stomach at the same time, while also dancing the fox-trot, doing math in your head and reciting poetry."

"I hope that's not the task," muttered Mickey. "There's no way I can do all that."

"That is not the task," said Nigel Cruul as if he'd overheard.

"Phew," I said.

"No," said Dominic. "Nigel is correct, that is not the task. The actual task is much more difficult than that."

"No, it isn't," sighed Cruul.

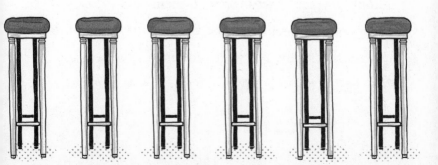

"Each of you –" continued Douglas, ignoring Cruul – "will take a stool. Music will be played. When you hear a key change you will rise from the stool. Then you will sit back down. Those that can't keep up will be eliminated."

"Seriously?" asked Annabelle. "That's your challenge? You want them to play reverse musical chairs?"

"Stool-manship is very important for a boy band," said Douglas.

"Maybe back in your day, old man," said Annabelle.

Douglas looked rattled. "The only reason stools aren't in right now is that most of the current groups can't work them. Men at Arms refuse to even be in the same building as them. And why do you think Bad Boyz are always in the papers for smashing stools onstage or setting fire to them or chucking them out of hotel windows? Because they can't work them, that's why. But we're looking for the best and the best boy bands have always been able to get on and off stools like no one's business. And it's my challenge so we're doing it."

Nigel Cruul sniggered as Annabelle rolled her eyes. "Whatever," she said.

A hand went up in the crowd.

"Yes?" asked Cruul, through the thinnest of smiles.

"Uh … yeah… Will we be singing to, like, actual music?"

Cruul looked confused. "Why on earth would you be singing? What a ridiculous question. Get out."

The boy looked horrified, but Cruul was insistent. "Go on, get out," he said. "If we wanted singing we'd have asked for it. Anyone else got any more dumb questions?"

There was silence, apart from the sobbing coming from the boy as he made his way to the exit.

"Good," said Cruul. "Now, let's get this nonsense over with."

We each took our positions. I had to admit the stool was pretty comfortable as far as stools went.

The music started to play. It was an instrumental of an Apocalips track called "You Are the One." It was one of the few Apocalips songs that I had been aware of before this last week. The song was voted the most inspirational song of all time, featuring in a gazillion TV ads where it inspired people to buy everything from cars to cat litter.

(Verse 1)

They tried to tell me, "Hey, you won't succeed,
Can't beat Usain Bolt, don't be stupiiiid."
So I got in my car and the race was brief.
Ain't called cheating, it's called self belief.

(Chorus) – Key Change Number 1

You can move mountains if you believe in yourself,
'Cause a mountain's just a rock that got a bit out
of hand.
Don't let them say that mountains are too big to be moved,
That it's totally impractical – they just don't understand.

(Verse 2)

You can do anything, it might just take a few tries.
Yeah, you can shoot laser beams out of your eyes.
Don't let them say you can't, they don't know.
Hang on to your dreams, babe, and don't let go.

(Chorus) – Key Change Number 2

(Verse 3)

People are going to tell you to listen to your head,
To be sensible and practical instead.
But life's too short to waste it thinking things through,
Just do what you want and hope that no one sues.

(Chorus) – Key Change Number 3

Because you can move mountains if you believe in yourself,
'Cause a mountain's just a rock that got a bit out
of hand.
Don't let them say that mountains are too big to be moved,
That it's totally impractical – they just don't understand.

They just don't

They just won't

Understand.

The first key change hit and everyone stood up in time, before sitting back down.

The second key change hit and everyone stood up in time, before sitting back down.

The final key change hit and this time … everyone stood up in time, before sitting back down.

The music ended. Nigel Cruul and Annabelle shook their heads.

"Oh," said Dominic. "I had thought more of you would struggle with that to be honest. Perhaps another round?"

"Oh, for heaven's sake, enough with this garbage. We'll never eliminate anyone at this rate," shouted Cruul, getting up from his chair and walking to the front of the stage. He pointed at a boy a few stools away. "Everyone to the left, including you, is eliminated."

There was uproar amongst the contestants. "B-b-but why?" whimpered the boy.

"Easy! We don't need unlucky people in

Apocalips," said Cruul.

Mickey and I remained where we were, too stunned to speak. We had been on the right side, in every sense of the word — Nigel Cruul had just eliminated everyone but five people. And we were among them.

APOCALIPS

CHAPTER SIXTEEN

★ ★ ★

"This is it," said Nigel Cruul. "The final task. At the end of this, one of you will walk out of here as the newest member of Apocalips. The rest of you will just walk out of here. Now I'll hand you over to Annabelle."

"We must have to sing now," whispered Mickey. For the first time since I had met him there was a clear tone of irritation in Mickey's voice. He was right, though. It had been incredible that we had made it to this point without singing – now had to be the time.

Right?

"The final round is your opportunity to show us your performance skills," said Annabelle. So definitely singing then, I thought, running my tongue over Milo's Sing-Sync to make sure it was still there. "As you know, I am one of the greatest performers of my generation. Or any generation, in fact. My standards are incredibly high, just as you will be today."

It quickly became clear to everyone what she meant by that. Behind us, offstage, five large platforms were being carefully wheeled out into the arena. A few black-clad crew members were gathered around one, testing it. They pressed a button, and the platform began to rise, higher and higher, until the column stretched some forty feet in the air.

"They're not expecting us to go on one of those?" asked a nervous-looking boy next to me.

"I think they probably are," I said as a microphone was thrust into my hand by a burly crew member.

Mickey's face lit up as he switched his on. "So, we'll be singing then?" he said into the mic.

"What? No," said Cruul. "Switch that thing off. What is it with you kids and your obsession with singing? That's not all this job is about, you know. Things go wrong singing live. As entertainment providers we need to be able to guarantee our customers … I mean fans, a good time, every time. Fans have high standards for their idols. Singing live can only end in disappointment. It can never match the quality of a studio recording. That's why Apocalips's live shows feature Simulated Vocal Performances™."

Mickey frowned. "You mean miming?"

Cruul sniffed indignantly. "Miming is for people who can't cut it as clowns," he said. "Apocalips provide Simulated Vocal Performances ™."

"Sounds like miming to me," muttered Mickey.

"Nothing *sounds* like miming," said Cruul. "That's the whole point of miming. Although it does sound like *you* might want to leave early."

Mickey appeared to be asking himself the same question, but after a few seconds seemed to think better of it and switched off his microphone.

"I thought as much," said Cruul.

Mickey looked furious, but this was great news for me. In a singing contest with no singing, I actually had a shot.

"Behind you," said Annabelle, "are five extending plinths. Now I know what some of you are thinking and the answer is yes: they are the same ones I used on my Lightning Mango tour. In this challenge, each of you will take your place on a platform which will be fully extended. An Apocalips track will then play, and it will be up to you to show us your performance skills by dancing and mim— er ... simulating vocals ... whatever it was that Nigel just said."

Annabelle clicked her fingers and a spotlight appeared on her. "Throughout the song, a spotlight, just like this one, will randomly shine on each of you. When that happens you have fifteen seconds to really show us what you can do. An individual performance where it's up to you to shine. Anyone who doesn't impress us gets buzzed, and you're out of here."

The lights came back up. "It's last boy standing," she said. "A fight to the death."

Dominic shook his head vigorously. "There will be no actual dying," he said. "You'll just have to go home."

"Which is even worse than death," insisted Annabelle.

"It's really not," said Dominic firmly.

As the two judges bickered, we made our way to the columns. I went for the one in the middle, and Mickey took the one to my left. I watched as the nervous boy seemed to be using every ounce of courage to step onto the column to my right. Sweat was pouring down his face. It was obvious his nerves had nothing to do with performing. The boy was terrified of heights. That became even clearer when the platforms began to rise.

"You'll be all right, the barrier will stop you falling," I shouted, pointing at the flimsy metal frame that surrounded the platform. If I was honest, I didn't think it looked that safe, but it was hardly going to help the situation by pointing that out. Not that it mattered, the boy couldn't hear me since the music had already started.

The track was called "Party Around the Clock" and was a song about partying around the clock. It was upbeat and felt like it had been scientifically designed to get people dancing. Which it probably had been.

I started to move in time to the beat, keeping it simple. I could see around me that the others were doing the same. Except for Nervous Boy, who was just holding on to the barrier for dear life.

Mom and Dad had taught me how to let my body feel the music. It had sounded lame to begin with, but once we had gotten into it, I began to understand. If the song was a sad ballad then you don't want a lot of movement. You make a face like you've just stubbed your toe, and then you either slap your chest a lot or mime squashing a tomato in your hand. But for a fast-tempo song like this, you need to let go a bit and trust your body to figure out what to do in the moment.

So that's why I was jumping around like the ground was made of hot coals. It wasn't pretty, but I knew I had to save what little moves I actually had for my fifteen seconds.

The lights went out, and a spotlight picked out the first column. It was like watching a deer caught in headlights, a deer that then had to pull off a sensational dance routine.

The boy, dressed in a Rolling Stones T-shirt and sporting hair that looked a bit like a tub of cress, panicked a little at first, unsure what to do. He then started throwing his hands in the air and making weird shapes. It was terrible. If this contest had been about skill and talent then this boy would have been eliminated some time ago. But instead it had all been sheer luck, and it looked like his had finally run out.

The shrill sound of three buzzers being pressed filled the arena. To the back of the stage, just behind the judges, three giant bulbs dangling from the rafters lit up bright red. The boy's column began to descend, and his dream was over.

Everyone carried on dancing, waiting for the next spotlight to fall. As the chorus kicked in, Mickey's column lit up.

Unlike the first boy, Mickey was ready. More than ready, in fact. He burst into a breathtaking routine, spinning and flipping in every possible direction, and finishing with a huge double backflip. It was incredible and, more importantly for Mickey, buzzer free. It was going to be hard to beat.

The spotlight fell next on the column farthest to my right. The boy here, obviously feeling the pressure from Mickey's performance, was flopping about like a fish trying to find a pond. It was pretty bad. It wasn't long before the three judges pressed their buzzers all at once. They hammered them so hard that the noise was even louder than before, and the red lights seemed to surge a little. Unfortunately for the boy, it also happened to be at the exact moment he was attempting a backflip. Distracted by the buzzers, he flipped himself right over the barrier and plummeted to the floor. Luckily a couple of security guards happened to be positioned beneath his column and broke his fall.

The judges laughed as the boy got to his feet and hobbled away. Nervous Boy looked more horrified than ever.

And then the light fell on me. It was time.

I went for it. It was like I became the Jittery Panda. The shakes, the jiggles, the shimmies, the wobbles, the bamboo eating – they were all perfect. I even nailed the upside-down bit.

Fifteen seconds later, it was over, and I was still in the competition. I looked over at Mickey, who was smiling at me. He gave me a nod, which I returned. But I knew that we'd both still have to go again,

until one of us slipped up. I'd
made it through one pass, maybe
I could make it through another
one or two, but a week's worth
of dance lessons wasn't going to
be enough against someone as
experienced as Mickey.

As I thought about my next
move, the spotlight fell on
Nervous Boy. His routine was
a little different. There were
no flips, no body-popping, no
elaborate choreography. There
was just vomit. Lots of vomit.
Moments before, the security
guards waiting below the
podiums had possibly guessed
that a teenage boy was the
absolute worst thing that would
fall on anyone that day. They
were wrong.

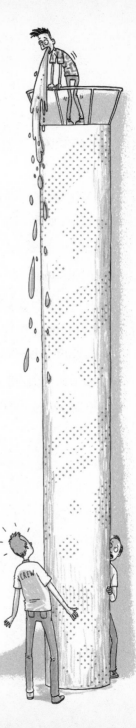

The judges began pounding their buzzers in outrage. They continued as Nervous Boy's platform lowered to the ground, and he sprinted out of the arena.

It appeared the judges had bashed the buzzers so hard they had overloaded the system. The giant red lights started to surge again, flickering violently and getting increasingly brighter until finally, all three exploded. Shards of glass fell to the stage, luckily too far behind the judges to injure anyone. But it wasn't just the buzzer lights that went out. The song cut out, the feed on the monitors disappeared, and the whole arena went dark.

APOCALIPS

CHAPTER
SEVENTEEN

★ ★ ★

A few moments later, the backup generator must have kicked in, and the lights came back on, although it looked like not everything had power as there was no sound coming through any of the speakers from the judges onstage. And from the way Nigel Cruul was throwing his arms around, he was definitely making a noise.

Mickey and I looked at each other with the same question etched on both our faces. *Now what?*

It was between us now, but without power it wasn't obvious how the competition could continue. Maybe they'd have to ask us to come back another day. I dreaded the thought of having to go through this again.

Then Mickey's voice boomed around the arena. "Testing, one, two."

I looked over at him. He was holding his microphone to his mouth, a mouth that had formed itself into a devilish smile. Whatever circuit the lights were on, the speakers for our microphones were on them, too. They obviously weren't on the same circuit as the judges, though, as Cruul waved furiously, but silently, at us.

Mickey didn't seem to care.

"There's only one way to settle this, Sam," he said, looking right at me. "A good old-fashioned sing-off. I'll go first."

Mickey didn't wait for me to reply, or pay any attention to Cruul screaming at the top of his lungs for him to stop as he launched into a cover of the Apocalips song "Fly Little Bird." It had recently been voted number one in a poll of the one hundred saddest songs of all time. Yet somehow Mickey made the song sound even sadder, his voice haunting and powerful. Annabelle and Dominic were openly crying, and even Cruul seemed to have a tear in his eye. I had never heard anything quite like it. It was incredible. It was amazing. It was a disaster.

As I watched Mickey put everything he had into it, I knew it was all over – the contest and the world. Nigel Cruul had appeared furious with Mickey when he started to sing, but he didn't seem mad anymore. My only hope was that once Mickey had finished, Cruul would disqualify him on the spot, and I wouldn't need to even open my mouth. But there was also a chance that if I didn't sing myself, the judges would automatically go with Mickey on account of him being so awesome.

I sighed. I wasn't getting away with it. I had to sing. It was too much of a risk not to. And at least if we both sang, Cruul surely wouldn't send us both home. He'd have to pick one of us.

"Milo?" I said, putting a hand over my mouth. "Are you there?"

No answer.

"Milo?" I repeated. "Milo?" I could hear the desperation in my own voice. What was I going to do? Without Milo's help I didn't stand a chance.

I had almost given up hope when I remembered what Milo had said outside the arena. The part about switching the Sing-Sync on.

I reached my tongue to the back of my teeth and clicked the little switch.

"Milo?"

"Sam?"

"Oh, thank goodness," I said, relieved to hear his voice.

"How's it going?" asked Milo.

"I've made the final two…" I started saying.

"The final two! Wow! That's amazing, I wasn't expecting that. Er… I mean, I was totally expecting that. Yes… This isn't a surprise at all. Ahem. Wait … you mean to tell me you've made it to the final two, and this is the first time you've been asked to sing? What's going on?"

"I don't know," I said. "None of this feels right, but that's what's happened. Listen, I need a song now. Something big."

"All right… From what I can hear through the Sing-Sync it sounds like the other guy's singing 'Fly Little Bird,'" said Milo. "And doing a great job with it."

"Right on both counts," I said.

"We're going to go the other way then," he said.

"What do you mean?"

"I mean, you're going to have to dance. Something energetic but not too out there."

"I've already done the Jittery Panda," I said.

"I don't know what that is, but it sounds gross…" said Milo. "Anyway, just figure something out."

I had no time to think as Mickey's song came to an end. I found myself clapping furiously along with the judges. Mickey mouthed "Thank you" and "Good luck" at me.

"All right, Milo, we're up," I said before switching on my microphone.

It was impossible to put into words how I felt over the following three minutes except that it was one of the most incredible moments of my life. As Milo promised, the song was the total opposite of Mickey's. "Summer Funk" was about as upbeat as you could get, and the vocal track that Milo had managed to dig out was incredible. For my part I was able to perform a fairly decent mash-up of the Evil Iguana and the Newcastle Bus Driver. For three minutes I was able to forget about the importance of actually winning in order to save the world and just enjoy the moment. I felt more alive in that small space of time than I had in my entire life. Was this what it felt like to actually be good at something?

When the song finished, Mickey and the judges were clapping. Apart from Nigel.

So that was it. Even with all the cheating I hadn't been good enough. It was over.

The arena was silent. Crew members handed a pale-looking Cruul and the rest of the judges microphones. I was guessing these ones actually worked.

"Those were both incredible performances. One in particular was extraordinary," said Cruul in a soft, slow voice. It was the same voice I had heard him use on TV shows before. It seemed designed to drag a moment out much longer than it needed to be, giving nothing away and keeping everyone in suspense. He was looking right at Mickey now. "I should send you straight home for that stunt you pulled. But I'm not going to."

Mickey looked stunned. He had done it. Under normal circumstances I would have been happy for him. Someone that talented deserved to win way more than someone like me. But these weren't normal circumstances, and I felt sick inside at the thought of failing.

"You, young man, made me feel like I've never felt before," continued Cruul. "The emotions, the sadness, I had all the feels, as they say nowadays. I've not felt like that in a long, long time."

"Thank you," said Mickey, looking genuinely touched.

Cruul's face turned sour. "It wasn't a compliment."

Mickey's face dropped. "Sorry?"

"I don't want to feel those things," said Cruul. "Apocalips fans don't want music to make them feel traumatized. They want to feel good. Even sad songs should make them feel good."

"Never in all my years in the business have I felt that awful after hearing a song," agreed Annabelle.

"I'm an emotional wreck right now," said an emotionless Dominic, whose tears from before were now nowhere to be seen.

"So no, we won't be sending you home for your

stunt," said Cruul. "But we will be sending you home because you aren't good enough."

The judges turned toward me.

"Congratulations, young man," said Nigel Cruul. "You are the new member of Apocalips."

APOCALIPS

CHAPTER EIGHTEEN

★★★

Cruul had barely finished his sentence when the power finally came back on.

"Now you all will actually hear me when I fire you!" he shouted at a group of nearby crew members, who immediately fled from his wrath.

The podiums were lowered to the ground, where several large men in suits quickly ushered me toward a side exit without saying a word. The judges were nowhere to be seen. As I was leaving, I glanced back and caught a brief glimpse of a dejected-looking Mickey. I hoped that one day I'd get a chance to explain to him what had happened.

Outside the arena I was bundled into an elevator. Minutes later I found myself standing in the middle of a large room filled with marble columns and crystal chandeliers and waiters in tuxedos serving champagne, while camera flashes blinded me in every direction. I was surrounded by smiling, glamorous-looking people I had never seen before. Actually that's not quite true. Some of the faces I recognized from TV and newspapers and magazines and who knows where else. Celebrities I sort-of-kind-of knew were looking at me as if I was the most important person in the world, laughing and backslapping and raising their glasses to me. An arm snaked its way around my shoulder as the smell of aftershave hit my nose like an uppercut.

"Here he is," said Nigel Cruul. "The newest member of Apocalips. Sammy!"

The room whooped and cheered at the mention of my almost-name.

"Actually, it's Sam…" I said, but no one seemed to hear.

A microphone was thrust into my face. "So, Sammy, what's it like being the newest member of Apocalips?" asked a woman I thought I recognized from interviewing celebrities on TV.

"It's … er … well, I haven't actually met them yet."

"All in good time," said Nigel.

"Your parents must be so proud," added the journalist.

"Oh, I should probably phone them and tell them," I said.

Nigel laughed. "Don't worry, we'll get the word out. All right, that's enough questions for now.

There'll be plenty of time for interviews later."

"Sammy, let me just say," said Dominic, shaking one of my hands with both of his, "your stool work out there was incredible. You're obviously classically trained."

"Er … no, I just—" I said before Annabelle shoved him out of the way.

"In my entire career I've never seen an audition as good as that," she said. "Word of advice, though, kid. If you're planning on lasting in this industry, the secret is to always be reinventing yourself. That's how I've lasted so long."

As I thanked her for the advice, a cold wind blew past me. Which was odd, given that we were indoors and there weren't any windows open. A round of applause broke out, but as heads turned to the far end of the room I could tell it wasn't for me. Slowly I turned around. The four members of Apocalips were standing in the doorway, their eyes trained on me.

"Guys, you're here," said Nigel Cruul, stating the obvious. He snapped his fingers and all the famous people, including Annabelle and Dominic, scurried out of the room.

The last time I had been this close to Apocalips, they had disintegrated another human being right in front of me, and I couldn't quite ditch this thought as Cruul led them over. What if they recognized me from the concert?

"We're ready to see the new blood," said Donnie, smiling darkly. Without thinking I took a step back.

"This is Sammy," said Cruul.

"It's … uh … Sam, actually," I said.

Cruul seemed to consider this, before shaking his

head. "No, Sammy is better."

"Oh. OK," I said.

"Well, he seems agreeable," said Pete from somewhere behind his mane of hair.

"Makes a change from the last guy," said Frankie, who looked even thinner in real life.

Warren, who had been staring menacingly at me the entire time, grunted. "Just wait until he gets a taste of fame. He'll go the same way, you see if he doesn't."

"I don't want to go the same way as Steve," I said.

"Yeah, I'll bet you don't," laughed Frankie, which prompted Warren to thump his bandmate on the arm. Frankie seemed to get the message and slinked away, clutching his arm.

"Now, now, boys, play nice," said Nigel Cruul. "Sammy here isn't going to rock the boat. He won't be a problem."

"Maybe so, but is he going to be ready for Hyde Park?" asked Donnie.

"Oh, he'll be ready," said Cruul. "He's got the hair, he can sing, he can dance, he can even get up off a stool. He's the full package."

The four of them shot Cruul a look of pure contempt and beckoned him over to a corner of the room. I had to strain to hear what was being said.

"What do you mean he can sing?" whispered Donnie. "How do you know that?"

"We gave you explicit instructions," muttered Warren. "No singing…"

"Yes, I know, I know," said Cruul. "But it was … unavoidable. Anyway, I still don't see what the big deal is. Just because he can sing doesn't mean he's going to quit like Steve did."

The four of them exchanged looks. That was interesting. Cruul didn't seem to be in on the fact that four members of his band had obliterated the fifth.

"The big deal is…" said Donnie, trailing off as he glanced over at me and seemed to realize that I could still hear them. "The big deal is that singers get big heads."

Donnie nudged the others. Whatever the real reason there wasn't supposed to be singing at the audition, I knew I wasn't going to find out now.

"Singers get ideas above their stations," said Pete.

"Singers forget their place," said Frankie.

"So I won't be singing?" I asked, trying not to sound relieved.

"That's the plan," grunted Warren.

Cruul didn't look especially pleased at this. "Is it?" he hissed. "Don't you think, as your manager, I should know the plan? I mean, you have to tell me these things."

The room suddenly got colder and the lights began to flicker. "*We don't have to do anything,*" said

Donnie, his voice sounding even deeper than before.

"No, no, of course not…" Cruul stuttered. "I just meant, Hyde Park is in two weeks. If he's not going to be singing… I mean … people will be expecting a performance."

The temperature and lights returned to normal and Donnie smiled. "Of course," he said. "And they'll get it. The singing will be covered, Nigel. Simulated Vocal Performances™, remember?"

"Miming, for this?" said Cruul, which seemed surprising given what he'd said about Apocalips's live shows at the audition.

"Trust us, Nigel," said Donnie. "Apocalips will give the world the performance of a lifetime."

"What's happening in Hyde Park?" I asked.

"He's asking too many questions," snapped Warren, taking a step toward me.

"That was only my second one," I said, backing away.

"Come on, Warren," Donnie said, stepping between us and giving me a smile. "Sammy here is one of us now. There should be no secrets among Apocalips. And besides, this isn't much of a secret. Hyde Park in London is the venue for our next concert. Over two hundred thousand Apocalips fans will gather to witness their idols deliver a spectacle to end all spectacles. And, as it happens, it will also be where the newest member – that's you – will make their live debut."

I gulped. "At the biggest concert of all time?"

"Yes," said Donnie. "Exciting, isn't it?"

I nodded weakly, feeling like I might throw up. Being tasked with saving the world was bad enough, but at that moment the thought of performing in front of a crowd that size seemed worse.

Donnie draped an arm around me. "Don't worry, you'll be fine," he said. "The singing isn't your concern. Being in a boy band requires so much more than being able to sing, and you did just great in all those other things we need. You're going to be a star, Sammy. And it begins right now."

Donnie led me to the far end of the room, flanked

by the rest of the band. Nigel Cruul ran in front of us and opened a huge pair of red velvet curtains, revealing a set of glass doors that opened out onto a balcony. Had Donnie not still had his arm around my shoulder, the roar that greeted us might have been enough to knock me over the ledge.

Thousands of people had gathered in the street below. The majority were women and young girls, but there were men and boys, too, all of them screaming their heads off. Donnie and Warren stood to my left, Pete and Frankie to my right. Suddenly my hands were being raised, and the crowd got even louder, the noise threatening to explode my eardrums. It was like electricity was flowing through me. Was this what it felt like to be famous?

Cruul's voice boomed from somewhere, announcing my name. Then the crowd was chanting. It was just a single word, over and over:

SAMMY-SAMMY-SAMMY-SAMMY!

It was no longer just my ears that were sore, my cheeks were, too – from the huge smile that had taken over my face. As I basked in the glory, waving to all my new fans, I had the faintest feeling that none of this was right. I was here to do something. Something important…

Then I remembered. I was here to be a star.

Sammy had finally arrived.

APOCALIPS

CHAPTER NINETEEN

★★★

Sammy's Band Diary

Sunday June 7th
One of the weirdest things about being a
star that no one ever mentions is how it
affects your memory. I know I won the
competition yesterday because everyone
keeps mentioning it, but I don't remember
much about it. Maybe it's because today was
so busy, but really the last thing I can recall
clearly was leaving the house last Saturday
to take Lexi and Amy to the Apocalips

concert. I'm not too worried though. I'm sure this is just me adjusting to becoming a huge celebrity. Even so, I've come up with an idea to help me keep track of things. Nigel gave me this notebook earlier. He says I'm to carry it with me at all times and to write down any useful notes he has for me during rehearsals (he has a lot of notes). But I've decided to also use it as a journal to try and keep track of what I've been doing in the run-up to our huge Hyde Park concert. Like a tour diary, I guess. Maybe when I'm old and retired I can read all these entries in the giant mansion that Nigel says I'll definitely have.

Nigel is so nice, by the way. He's not at all like the cold-blooded shark he comes across as on TV. He's lovely to everyone, except for anyone not in the band or me when I make a mistake, which is a lot of the time. But if I'm not making a mistake, he doesn't shout at me at all.

The rest of the band are a little distant, if I'm honest. I don't want to say that I think they're hiding something from me because that sounds terribly paranoid. I think it's just that they have their thing going on, and I'm the new guy, and none of us has really figured out how to fit together yet. At the end of the day they're an amazing group of guys. I'm so privileged just to be around them.

Monday June 8th

I had my first TV interview today. Well, actually, I had my first dozen TV interviews today. Not just TV, either - radio, newspapers, magazines, bloggers, it was like everyone wanted to meet me! It was so much fun, although it did get a bit repetitive after a while as everyone asked the same questions.

What's it like to be the newest member of Apocalips? Amazing, obviously.

Are you looking forward to making your live debut at Hyde Park? Of course I am!

How are you adjusting to the new lifestyle? There's still so much to take in. I haven't quite gotten used to it yet, but I'm so lucky to have the support of my new bandmates and manager.

Nigel really is supportive. He made sure he gave me all the answers to everyone's questions ahead of time so I didn't have to worry about a thing.

Oh, and I've stopped wearing that retainer. My teeth are fine. I really have no idea why I was wearing it in the first place.

Tuesday June 9th
Lots of training today in preparation for next week's concert. I'm finding it easier and easier to remember all the dance moves now. For some reason I felt gratitude toward my parents for this. No idea why. I mean I love

them, but they're a couple of accountants who'd probably rather watch Strictly Financing than Strictly Come Dancing. I haven't actually spoken to them since Saturday morning. Nigel has spoken to them, of course - he's gotten all the permissions I need to take off school. He's passed along messages from them congratulating me, but he'd rather I wait till after the concert before I speak to anyone from what he calls my "old" life, including Lexi and Milo. Ha! I wonder what Milo thinks of me making the band. Can't remember if I even told him I was auditioning. Anyway, Nigel doesn't want me distracted, which makes sense. I definitely don't need distractions.

Wednesday June 10th
More practice and interviews today. I should mention the hotel I'm staying in. Nigel's label owns the Dahlington Grande. We've basically taken over the whole thing as our base.

The suite I'm staying in is amazing. It has everything you can think of:

- The biggest, comfiest bed I've ever slept in. It's so big that I've never actually made it to the other side. I assume it has one, but I can't actually say for sure.
- All the latest games consoles, with every game ever released for them. And even some that haven't been.
- All the faucets have three settings - hot, cold and cola.
- As well as a regular fridge, there's a chocolate fridge. As in, it contains nothing but chocolate, not that it's made out of chocolate.
- There's also a fridge made out of chocolate.

Thursday June 11th
I'm starting to get used to hotel life! I can use the swimming pool whenever I feel

like it or eat in the restaurant no matter what time of day or night. They'll cook me anything I ask for. This morning I had a chocolate, vanilla and bacon ice cream sundae for breakfast. Not as nice as it sounds. The only place I'm not allowed to go is the 28th floor. The rest of the band don't want me going up there. I'm not sure why, but this morning I did overhear a couple of the hotel staff talking about not going up there. Didn't catch it all, but I'm sure I heard Steve's name being mentioned so I think that might be the floor he used to stay on.

I think the band are still hurting from him leaving, and maybe it's too soon for them to see me in his old surroundings. Maybe in the future things will get easier for them, and they'll get a bit of perspective. After all, Steve leaving isn't exactly the end of the world. I mean, it's not like he's dead!

Friday June 12th

You'll never believe what I got my hands on today. The brand-new Apocalips album. It's still under embargo, so not even sure I'm allowed to write this down. Ah, what's the harm? It's called *Prophecies* and it's going to drop the day of the concert. Sorry, "drop" is a music industry term for release. I don't know why they don't just say that, I guess "drop" sounds cooler. I'm rambling here, I'm just so excited. The cover is divided into four sections, with the faces of Donnie, Warren, Frankie and Pete taking up a section each. I'm not that bothered that I'm not on there - Nigel says they didn't have time to add me. Though presumably they had time to take Steve off. The album is so good. I've heard a few songs from it already of course, but just the ones we're going to be performing at the concert. This was my first time hearing the entire thing. No one's going

to read this anyway so I guess I can write
down the track listing:

1. Before There Was Anything
2. Time and Space
3. The Reckoning
4. Until the End
5. We Roam the Earth
6. Nothing Can Stop Us
7. The Child with the Voice of Light
8. Not Who We Say We Are
9. Death and Destruction
10. The Last Ride

Bonus Track: Unchained Melody

It's a bit heavy going at times to be
honest (except for "Unchained Melody," which
is just a sublime cover version), but "The Child
with the Voice of Light" really speaks to me
for some reason.

Saturday June 13th
It's less than a week now to Hyde Park.

Today we were working on the big final number. People are going to go crazy for this. The plan is that the five of us will ride out on horses, singing "The Last Ride." I've never ridden before and definitely not while performing the closing track to the biggest concert of all time. But if we pull this off it's going to be epic. The only problem, and it's such a small problem that I feel bad even mentioning it, is that technically I'm not actually riding a horse. Nigel says that he's still trying to track down a suitable fifth horse for me, so in the meantime I'm stuck with Polly the pony. I'm sure Nigel will have it sorted out before Saturday, although I think he might have trouble finding a horse as striking as the ones the rest of the band are using.

Seriously, you've never seen animals like these. Each horse is a different color – Warren's is red, Pete's is white, Frankie's is black and Donnie's is a pale green.

They're so powerful and intimidating, honestly, if I didn't know better I'd almost think they weren't of this world. Polly, on the other hand, is definitely from this world. She's about as pony-like as a pony can get.

Sunday June 14th

It's a little after three in the morning. I've just woken up. I can't think straight. I had a dream about the horses. Hooded figures were riding them toward me, and I was running but not fast enough. They were about to trample me... And now I keep thinking I'm supposed to be doing something. Something important. But every time I try to remember what it is, the memory vanishes. I reach out to grab it, and it slinks back into the darkness of my mind. I know this sounds crazy, but I feel that if I don't remember this soon something really, really bad is going to happen. It's like all the pieces are right in front of me, but I can't put any of them together. I wish Milo were here, he'd be able to help make sense of all this. I need to...

I need to...

I need to work on my routines. There's only five days to go, and I still haven't gotten the opening song down yet.

Monday June 15th

Everything's really coming together. Obviously I'm still totally nervous about making a good impression on the Apocalips fans, but I am quietly confident that I've got all the routines now. I can't wait to set foot onstage and show everyone what I can do—

APOCALIPS

CHAPTER TWENTY

★ ★ ★

"What's wrong with him, Milo?"

"I don't know but he's got those same glassy eyes that you had."

"Lexi, Milo," I said. I was standing next to them in the middle of my hotel room, not entirely sure how I had gotten there.

"Sam, are you all right?" asked Milo. "You seem … zoned out. We had to pull you away from that notebook. You weren't answering us. You were just sitting there writing."

"Writing…" I said. "Yes … I have to write … have to remember… I'm Sammy not Sam, you know."

Lexi and Milo looked at each other. "Yeah, I'm not calling you that," said Lexi.

"Have you come to see the show?" I asked. "It's not till Saturday. You really shouldn't be here. Nigel wouldn't like it. I'm not to be distracted."

"This is pretty bad," said Milo. "He actually thinks he's in the band. As in, really in it."

"I am in the band," I said.

"Yeah, but do you remember why you're in the band?" he asked.

What a silly question that was. "I won the competition," I said. "I was the best."

"Do you think it might help if I slap him?" asked Lexi.

Milo shook his head. "It might help you, but I don't think it'll help him. He's obviously under some kind of trance, like the one you were under. Which means we know how to break it."

A trance? I wasn't under a trance. I think I'd know if I was under a trance.

"Yeah, but how exactly?" asked Lexi. "We can't

just do the same thing that worked for me."

They were talking about me as if I wasn't there. I didn't really have time for this. I had to… I had to… What was I doing again?

Milo slapped his forehead. "You're right. Well, I guess we'd better leave Sam in peace then. Oh… Sam, before we go, the Heatherstones asked me to get your autograph."

That's right, I was writing in my journal…

"Sorry?" I said. "What about the Heatherstones?"

"Well 'asked' is probably the wrong word," said Milo. "'Told' is probably more accurate. Or 'threatened.'"

"They … want my autograph?" I spluttered.

"Said I'd better not come back without it," said Milo. "Oh yeah, they're big fans of yours now. I saw Vicky kissing a poster of you. She wasn't even trying to hide it."

Suddenly the room began to spin. A spark ignited in my brain causing thoughts and memories to start shooting through my head like fireworks.

I could
still hear Milo
talking. "I'm
lucky it's just an
autograph I need.
They were talking about
trying to get me to arrange
a date with one of them. Imagine
that, you going out with a Heatherstone."

The fireworks in my head turned into missiles,
overwhelming me with images of life before
Apocalips. Milo, my sister, my parents…

"Honestly, they were having this big argument
about which one of them would get to marry you!"

I felt my body go limp, and then Milo and Lexi's
arms were grabbing me and placing me gently onto
the bed. And I remembered everything.

I remembered.

Me.

Sam.

CHAPTER TWENTY-ONE

I threw my arms around them both. For the first time since the audition my head felt clear. For over a week it had been like I was watching myself from a distance, while someone else played my part. Somehow I was back. And so was my memory of why I was here. The ever-so-small matter of the world being destroyed by a crazed boy band.

I grabbed Lexi's head with both arms and stared into her eyes. I had to be sure it was my sister in there.

"Get off," she said, shoving me away. "Yes, it's me, not Zombie Lexi."

Milo was grinning.

"You brought her back?" I asked. "Like you brought me back? Wait, how did you bring me back exactly?"

Milo stopped grinning. "I … er … learned a counter spell," he said.

"Tell me," I said. "This is important. If you've found a way to break this hold Apocalips has on people then maybe we have a chance to stop them."

"We don't really have to go into that now," said Milo, shifting uncomfortably.

"Tell me," I repeated.

"Milo didn't break the spell," said Lexi. "You did."

"Me?" I said, more confused than ever. "What did I do? I've been with the band for the past week."

Lexi and Milo seemed to be growing more awkward by the second. "Er … yeah," said Lexi. "That's sort of what did it, to be honest."

I looked to Milo for an explanation. "OK…" he said, clearing his throat. "So it's like this. It turns out that whatever the hold is that Apocalips has on people, it can be broken by the same thing that's always been able to bring down boy bands."

Milo was looking at me as if it was obvious. All I could offer was a shrug.

"Three words," said Milo. "NBC – Not Being Cool. Somehow the spell only seems to work so long as the victim thinks Apocalips are cool. That's why I told you that the Heatherstones were in love with you. I guessed it would make being in the band seem a thousand times more lame. And it worked."

I nodded slowly. "So … the Heatherstones don't want to marry me?"

"I don't know," he said. "They might. No one's seen them in ages. Someone said they're camped outside Apocalips headquarters, though we didn't see them on the way into the hotel. You might want to be on the lookout, just in case."

"Good idea," I said, turning to Lexi. "That explains *me,* but I still don't understand what I had to do with *you*. Oh … wait a minute…"

Lexi's face had already turned a little pink.

"It was me joining the band, wasn't it?" I said, shooting her a frown. "As soon as your brother became part of Apocalips they suddenly seemed, what was it, a thousand times more lame?"

My sister's pink face darkened into a vibrant red. "Sorry," she said.

As much as I was relieved to have my sister back, it stung to think it was only because she was embarrassed by her big brother being a pop star. Then I remembered that moment back in our house where Lexi had seemed to come out of the trance for a moment. It was right after I told her I was auditioning. So even just the thought of me joining the band was enough to break the hold, if only for a few seconds. Wonderful.

"How did you guys even get in here?" I asked. "This place is like a fortress."

"Interesting you should ask," said Milo, but before he could continue, there was a knock on the door.

"Sammy," shouted Nigel Cruul. "Sammy, open up."

"Quick," I whispered, "get under the bed."

The pair of them dived beneath it.

I took a second to compose myself. I knew that when I opened the door, to avoid suspicion, I would have to act like the same weirdo I had been for the last week. I took a deep breath and pulled the handle. "**Yo, Nige, wassup?**"

Yo, Nige? Well, I'd get full marks for being weird, I guess.

Nigel looked at me with disgust. "Has anyone knocked on your door this evening?" he said.

"Yes," I said. "You. Just now."

Nigel closed his eyes and rubbed his temple. "Apart from me. Obviously."

"Oh," I said. "No. Why?"

"There's been some kind of break-in," he said. I could see his eyes darting around the room. "The security guard at the front desk was just found tied up in a sack in a broom closet. Unfortunately he didn't see who did it, and somehow all the cameras in the building were turned off for about five minutes, which was when the security guard was ambushed."

"Wow," I said. "Is Gary OK?"

Nigel looked at me blankly. "Who's Gary?"

"The security guard," I said.

"Oh, is that his name?" said Cruul, looking completely uninterested.

"Aren't you godfather to his son?" I asked.

Nigel sighed. "I'm godfather to a lot of people's sons," he said. "I can't be expected to remember them all. And yes, he's fine. I mean, obviously, he's fired but apart from that… So you haven't seen or heard anyone? Other than me?"

I shook my head.

Nigel's eyes made one final sweep of the room before he turned away. "Good. Most likely some overzealous fans trying to meet the band, but we can't be too careful, especially not this close to the show. If anyone does show up, raise the alarm at once."

"Will do," I said, watching with relief from the doorway as Cruul walked back toward the elevator.

"Oh, and Sammy?" he said, jabbing one of the elevator buttons.

"Yes?" I said as the door pinged and opened.

"Don't ever call me 'Nige' again," said Cruul, stepping inside.

"Sorry, Nigel," I shouted.

"*Sorry, Nigel*," said Lexi sarcastically as she and Milo crawled out from under the bed.

"Be quiet," I said. "What is it with you and sacks, by the way?"

My sister shrugged. "Hey, if you have a talent, why deny it?" she said.

"You think it's a talent, shoving people into sacks?" I asked.

"Well, I definitely couldn't do it," put in Milo. "Could you?"

I had to admit, he had a point. "And I take it the cameras going down was you?" I asked him.

Milo gave a little bow, then took out a mobile

phone from his pocket. "Easy when you know how. I wrote an app that can hack into most security camera channels. It lets me watch the feed on my phone while disabling it for everyone else. That's why we were able to sneak past everyone undetected. Well, mostly undetected. Your pal Gary was a bit of a problem, until your sister got involved."

"Yeah, well, you got him fired," I said.

"I did him a favor then, didn't I?" said Lexi. "Now he doesn't have to work for people plotting to destroy the world."

Again I was forced to admit that she had a point there.

"So have you made any progress in stopping that from happening?" asked Milo. "The destruction of the world, I mean."

"No," I said. "They had me under their spell from the moment I won the competition. Hey, that's a point, I never even got a chance to thank you for that song you played to help me win.

Wherever you downloaded it from, it was perfect."

Milo gave me an odd look. "Downloaded?" he said curtly. "Is that what…? Hang on, you're not wearing the retainer."

I ran my tongue along the top of my teeth. "Right, yeah," I said. "In the trance I couldn't remember what it was for, so I took it out. I left it next to my bed."

I pointed toward the bedside table, but the device wasn't there. Then I noticed the wastepaper basket on the floor beside it. "Oh. Maybe I knocked it into the trash. The housekeeper must have taken it."

"Perfect," said Milo, biting his lip. "It's not like I spent days working on that or anything…"

"I'm sorry, I—"

"Let's just concentrate on coming up with a plan," he said, cutting me off. "Do you have any information that might help us? What about that book you were writing in?"

"Book? Oh yeah, my journal. I started writing it right after I joined the band. I decided to keep a record of my days just to try and get things straight in my head, but I never could."

"Well, maybe you wrote down something useful in there," said Milo, in an impatient tone.

"Yeah, maybe," I said, picking up the journal only for Milo to snatch it from my hands.

Frowning, he took it over to the desk in the corner of the room and began flicking a little too aggressively through the pages. He definitely seemed annoyed about something. I turned to Lexi for an explanation.

"Come on, Sam," she whispered. "Do you honestly think that was a recording he was playing at the audition?"

I felt like I was missing something obvious here. If it wasn't a recording then the only other alternative was...

"Milo sang it himself?" I whispered back. It sounded absurd to say it, but Lexi was nodding.

"Milo?" I said.

Lexi nodded.

"That Milo?" I said, pointing toward him.

"Yes," she whispered.

"Singing? Our Milo? The one over there, right now? Singing? An actual song? Milo? Him over there?"

"Yes, Sam," snapped Lexi. "That Milo over there. Our Milo. He can sing, Sam. He's amazing."

I nodded. "Well … yeah, I know… I heard. Wow! It didn't even occur to me that it might be him. He's just normally so … Milo-ish."

I remembered my parents had a similar reaction when I told them I was auditioning. Except in Milo's case, he actually had talent.

"Shy people can sing, too, you know," said Lexi.

She was right, of course, but this was a side of Milo I had never seen before, and it was hard not to be shocked. You would have thought that my accountant parents being secret former pop stars would have taught me that people can always surprise you. "I should apologize," I said.

"You think?" she said, giving me a look that said,

Of course you should, you doofus. Milo suddenly leaped up from the desk and rushed toward us.

"Milo, I'm so sorry. I had no idea you were such an amazing singer," I said. "Why didn't you tell me?"

Milo blushed a little, before waving me away. "It doesn't matter. Look, I found something." He pointed at the entry from last Thursday. "What's on the 28th floor?"

I looked at the entry. "Like it says, I don't know," I said. "I'm not allowed up there, remember?"

Milo rubbed his chin, lost in thought. "They must have something up there," he said. "Something big, I'm guessing."

"That's not much to go on," said Lexi.

"You're right," agreed Milo. "All right, what do we know for certain then? We know that no one's allowed on the 28th floor."

"And we know about Hyde Park," I said. "It's going to be the biggest concert ever. Maybe that's when whatever they're planning will go down."

"Yeah, we sort of guessed that much," said Milo.

"You did?"

Milo nodded. "It's all anyone's talking about," he said. "They're calling it a once-in-a-lifetime event. If I was a crazy boy band who wanted to destroy the world, I'd definitely do it then."

"Two hundred thousand Apocalips fans are going to that thing," said Lexi. "That's a lot of people to work their evil mojo on. They could have their own army."

Milo nodded. "Lexi gave me a list of all the girls that had been patrolling the streets with her. Every single one of them had been to an Apocalips concert. Their power seems to only affect people who have seen them live."

"Or been in contact with them directly," I said, remembering how it felt like electricity was passing through me when the band took my hands on the balcony after the audition.

"Exactly," said Milo. "From your diary, it sounds like the last song is important. Not sure what the horses are about, I'll need to do a bit more research there. But I really want to know what's on the 28th floor… Wait a minute…"

Milo took out his phone again and began tapping away at the screen. "OK, I've bought up the camera feed."

The three of us crowded around the little screen. Unfortunately there wasn't an awful lot to see. The camera was fixed on a door, in front of which stood two huge, mean-looking men in suits.

"Try one of the other cameras," said Lexi. "Inside the room would be nice."

"There are no other cameras on that floor," said Milo. "It looks like that's the only room, too. You're going to have to find out what they're keeping in there," said Milo.

I nodded before realizing what he'd just said. "Me?" I asked. "Aren't you going to help?"

"We have to get back," said Lexi. "Mom and Dad will be expecting us. Sorry, I mean Cat and D!"

"They know you're here?" I said, finding that hard to believe.

"Of course," smiled Lexi. "Milo told them that he had spoken to Nigel Cruul and convinced him to let you take a break from rehearsing for half an hour to see your sister and best friend."

"So it has to be you," continued Milo. "Just keep an eye on the door. Maybe they don't watch it all the time. If you see a chance to get in, take it."

"How exactly am I going to watch the door?" I asked.

"Whoops, almost forgot," said Lexi, reaching into her pocket. She took out a shiny black phone and handed it to me. "From Mom and Dad. Give them a call soon, they really miss you. I think Cruul keeps having his secretary give them the runaround."

I looked at the phone. It was funny to think that everything that had happened to me was because I had wanted it so badly. Now it didn't seem like a big deal at all. Not when I couldn't be sure the world was going to last past Saturday.

"I took the liberty of preloading my app on your phone," said Milo. "It's got a record feature, too. It'll upload the camera footage to a cloud server so you'll be able to watch those guards day and night and see if they have any patterns – like when they go for breaks and stuff. Meanwhile, we'll do what we can from our end. I'll look into those horses and the track listing. I might hang on to your journal, too, if that's all right?"

"Yeah, no problem," I said.

"And I'll continue on Project Apocasux," said Lexi proudly.

"Project what?" I asked.

Milo sighed. "She's spending her time bad-mouthing Apocalips on internet forums."

"I'm creating a backlash," she explained. "If I can turn people off going to the concert in the first place, problem solved. And it's not just forums. I've set up Facebook pages, Twitter accounts and e-petitions."

"And how's that going?" I asked.

"Well, I'm pretty much banned from the internet now," she said. "So I'm mostly just phoning in anonymously to radio stations."

"I guess every bit helps," I said, not convinced my sister's trolling tactics would really do much to prevent the Apocalypse. "Are you guys going to be OK getting out of here? Nigel's probably got more people patrolling the building by now."

"Pfft," said Milo. "They didn't see us come in, they won't see us go out. We're like ghosts."

"And if they do see us then I'll knock their blocks off," said Lexi, shaking her fists.

Just as I was thinking how good it was to have my sister back to normal, she was gone and Milo with her. Now it was down to me, armed only with a smartphone, to stop Apocalips and save the world.

APOCALIPS

CHAPTER TWENTY-TWO

★ ★ ★

Saturday arrived, the dawn light creeping from behind the curtains as I lay on top of my bed, staring at the images on my phone of the two security guards standing in front of the mysterious door on the 28th floor. I had been worried at first that being near Apocalips again would put me back under their spell, but I couldn't see them now without thinking about the Heatherstones. It was hard to imagine any spell more powerful than the thought of being married to one of those harpies. So I had a fully functioning brain to think of a plan to bring the band down from the inside. And so far I had come up with nothing.

In the days after Lexi and Milo's visit, most of my time was spent with Apocalips, rehearsing for the show. Pretending I was still under their spell wasn't as hard as I'd expected. As long as I did what I was told, when I was told, they didn't seem to take much notice of me.

In the brief moments I had to myself, I watched the video footage, skipping through it to try and find something, anything, that I could use to get into the room. But the guards only ever budged when they were being relieved of their shift by two other guards, and there was no other way in as far as I could see. It was hopeless.

And now it was the day of the show and possibly the last day on earth, unless I could work out how to get into that room. I thought about everyone I might never see again – Lexi, Milo, my parents. I had called them the night Lexi gave me the phone. They had been so proud. Dad kept telling me about all the new dance moves he had been coming up with since I made the band, and Mom said she'd been hitting up most of the karaoke bars in town. In disguise, of course, but she had never been brave enough even for that before. They said they were inspired by me. Inspired? I was just as much of a fraud as Apocalips. I had cheated my way into the band, and now I couldn't even figure out how to get into a room.

I had only spoken to Milo a couple of times since his visit. His investigation into the horses and the lyrics had led to nothing but dead ends. The room was still our only lead.

"Baby, baby, baby, baby, baby."

I almost dropped my phone in fright, forgetting that I had set an alarm to make sure I didn't sleep in. I grinned, realizing that Lexi must have set the alarm tune as a twisted joke before giving it to me.

I took one last look through the footage, skipping back to this time yesterday morning. I couldn't believe it. There it was: a way in. Maybe. I checked the previous morning's footage, too, and there it was again. It had been right there in front of me, but somehow it had taken that annoying song for all the pieces to slot into place.

I switched the footage back to the live feed. Good. I hadn't missed my window. But I'd have to move fast. I quickly got dressed and slipped out of my room. It was still a little early for most people to be up, but I knew it wouldn't be long before the Dahlington Grande would be a hive of activity.

I had no choice but to take the stairs. Even if I could have taken the elevator, it was too risky. There were ten floors between me and the 28th floor; someone was bound to get in who recognized me. And I didn't have my sister's skill for tying people up in sacks to fall back on.

Three weeks ago I probably would have passed out around floor 23. But due to all the exercise I'd been doing lately, I made it to the top barely breaking a sweat. As I reached the 28th floor I could hear two voices.

"Hey, you ever wonder what's behind this door?" asked the first.

"Nope," said the second. "I don't get paid to think about that."

"Well, obviously you don't get paid to think about that. That's a ridiculous thing to pay someone for."

"Exactly."

"Yeah, but even so, you must have thought about it."

"Nope."

"Seriously? You've been standing outside this door for weeks now, and you've never once wondered to yourself what might be in there. It's never crossed your mind?"

"Nope. Lots of things don't cross my mind."

"Like what?"

"Like if I'm beating up a work colleague who asks too many questions, it never crosses my mind that he might want to walk again."

There was a long silence until finally the first voice said quietly, "Whatever it is, it's probably terrible anyway."

A few more seconds passed, then I heard the ping I was waiting for, followed by a low rumbling sound. Someone had just come out of the elevator.

"Morning, Betty," said the two men.

"Morning, lads," replied Betty.

I peeked out of the stairwell for a second. A woman wearing a light-blue dress and a white apron was pushing a large cart full of cleaning equipment down the hall. Betty the housekeeper. Regular as clockwork. And my only hope.

"Still don't understand why they get you up here," said the first man. "There's only one room and no one's allowed in it."

"Got to vacuum these hall carpets, haven't I?" replied Betty as the cart rumbled toward me. There was a pause. "Oh no. I've only gone and left the vacuum downstairs. Every day I forget that thing. What am I like? Oh well, back down I go."

Despite the fact that Betty looked like my gran, I could have kissed her. As she disappeared back into the elevator, I could see she had left her cart in the middle of the corridor, right between me and the guards.

It was now or never. I held my breath and, keeping low, I slipped into the hall and ducked behind the cart. As quietly as I could, I began moving it slowly back toward the two men, making sure to keep myself hidden.

Another couple of feet and I was exactly where I needed to be. Bringing the cart to a stop, I carefully reached inside and took out a can of air freshener. Taking aim at the fire alarm directly above me, I pressed the nozzle, hoping that the film I had seen this work in once before was factually accurate.

WEEE-WEEE-WEEE-WEEE-WEEE!

"What's that?" asked the first guard as I ducked back down behind the cart.

"Fire alarm, obviously," said the second. Through a narrow gap between the cart and the wall I could see him striding in my direction.

"Where are you going?" called the first guard.

"I don't get paid to get burned to death," replied the second as he hurried past me and down the stairs.

"Are you sure?" shouted the first. "Those contracts were a bit vague when it came to that. But we're definitely not supposed to leave this door under any circumstances. Do you smell air freshener?"

There was no reply. The second guard was probably halfway down the stairs by now.

After a few seconds, the first guard shrugged. "Wait for me," he shouted before breaking into a sprint.

I rushed over to the door. My first thought was that it would surely be locked, but when I turned the handle, it gave a little click and the door swung open.

Inside was this:

Nothing.

Well, nothing that I could see. The room was in total darkness. I stepped inside, hoping to find a light switch. But as I went to place my hand on the wall, I realized there was no wall anymore. It had gone.

Suddenly a light came on. I was standing in the middle of what looked like a large cave. The walls and ground were a reddish rock and stalactites hung from the ceiling. I glanced behind me at the door, which now gave off an uncanny green glow.

Then it swung shut and vanished. In the center of the room was a bed. A huge flat-screen TV was mounted on one of the walls. There was a wardrobe. And a fridge. And there were pizza boxes scattered everywhere. Whatever this place was, *wherever* it was, someone was staying here, as if it were just another of the hotel's suites.

I walked around the room, trying to find
something that might explain any of this.

FLUSH!

The noise came from behind me. I spun around
just in time to see a door form in the rock wall.
It swung open and out walked a familiar-looking
teenage boy, dressed in a pair of Apocalips pajamas.

The boy froze when he saw me. We stood there
staring at each other for what felt like forever.

"Well, this is awkward," said Steve.

APOCALIPS

CHAPTER TWENTY-THREE

★★★

"You really shouldn't be here," said Steve, smiling nervously.

There was no doubt it was him. The picture of him on his pajamas was giving me the very same grin.

"I … I … shouldn't be here?" I asked. "You're the one who shouldn't be here. You're supposed to be … well … dead."

"Actually, I'm supposed to be in hiding," Steve said. "Which, I think you'll agree, is clearly what I'm doing."

"But … I saw them… I saw them … obliterate you," I said.

Steve cocked an eyebrow, looking at me with interest. "So … you were convinced I was dead?"

"A giant ball of fire swallowed you up," I cried. "Of course I thought you were dead."

Steve looked momentarily delighted but then seemed to remember himself and put on a serious face. "I'm not supposed to be talking to you," he said. "I'm not supposed to be talking to anyone, actually, but especially not you."

"No, he's not."

I spun around to see Donnie standing there, smiling menacingly at me. Behind him stood Warren, Frankie and Pete, who weren't smiling but looked no less menacing for it.

"I didn't tell him anything, Donnie," said Steve as he scurried away from me.

"I know, Steve," said Donnie. "You did good. We're only here because when a fire alarm gets set off on the 28th floor we're probably going to look into that. I'm afraid Sammy here is more inquisitive than we gave him credit for."

"The name's Sam, not Sammy," I said, clenching my fists.

"Oooooh," said Frankie, rubbing his palms together. "Our Sammy's finally grown a backbone."

"Check out his little fists," said Warren.

"Maybe he's a fighter after all, like that sister of his," said Pete.

"What do you know about my sister?" I snapped. The four of them had never even met Lexi, as far as I knew, and I planned on keeping it that way.

"We know lots about you, Sammy," said Donnie. "We've been following you your entire life."

I looked at the four of them. They weren't that much older than me. "Since you were babies?" I asked.

Donnie rolled his eyes. "Of course not since we

were babies," he said. "We have never been babies. We existed before there was anything, before time and space themselves."

"It was great," said Frankie, staring longingly into the distance.

"Yeah," said Pete. "No humans, no planets, no anything."

"And now, after billions of years," continued Donnie, "we will finally return to a state of nothingness. There will be a reckoning."

Then the four of them spoke in unison: "Until the end, we roam the earth. Nothing can stop us."

This was all somehow familiar. Then I remembered. They were quoting song titles at me from the new album, *Prophecies*.

"So they're actual prophecies, the tracks from the album?" I asked.

Donnie smiled. "That was my idea," he said. "I thought it would be a nice touch to release the Doomsday Prophecies as a pop album. Our fans will buy anything with our name on it."

"That's because they're under your control,"
I said. "Like I was."

Donnie's smiled disappeared. "Oh, Sammy,
you don't get it, do you? You were never under our
control. The spell you were under was called fame.
Once you had a taste you were hooked, like humans
always are."

I gasped. I remembered back to the balcony
and seeing all those people cheering for me. I'd
felt overwhelmed with love and adoration, and
above all I'd wanted to always feel that way. Had
the desire to be famous taken me over? Had the
feeling of electricity flowing through my body,
the haze I fell into, all simply been the feeling of
becoming a star, rather than some kind of spell?

The four band members started laughing.

"Nah, I'm just messing with you," said Donnie.
"You were totally under our control from the
moment we all linked hands."

I shut my eyes and let out a deep breath. I really
hated these guys.

"Congratulations on breaking free, Sammy," said Donnie, giving me a patronizing little clap. "I thought it'd take you much longer, if you ever did at all. Now, I imagine you've probably got questions for us. Well, let's see if we can answer them."

Frankie looked concerned. "Wait, we're just going to let him ask questions?"

"He's no danger to us now," Donnie reassured him. "And besides, we've spent centuries building up to today. If we don't tell him then no one will ever know about all the work we put in. What's the point in that?"

"I agree, it was a lot of effort," said Pete. "What about all the paperwork we had to fill out to get that permit for Hyde Park?"

Donnie rolled his eyes. In fact, they rolled all the way around, which made me flinch. "I'm not talking about the admin, you idiot," he snapped. "I meant our plans, our plots, our schemes! He'll want to know about them, won't he?"

He was right. I had so many questions, but where

to even start? Then I realized: start at the beginning. "What really happened to Steve?" I asked, glancing over at Steve who instantly looked away, pretending to be distracted by a loose thread on his pajamas.

"Good question," said Donnie. "Of course you probably figured out that we didn't kill him."

I nodded. I had at least gotten that much.

"You'll be pleased to learn that it was all about you, Sammy," said Donnie, that horrible smirk returning to his pale face. "You, who've never been particularly good at anything. Your annoying little friend Milo, well, he's practically a genius, and your sister may be one of the greatest warriors we've ever seen."

"And we've known Genghis Khan," added Pete.

"And I assume your parents have told you about their pop star past," Donnie continued. "Surrounded by such talented people must be hard for you. I bet you've always wanted to be special, haven't you? So envious of the obvious talents of others, it probably never occurred to you how

245

important you are. But now you're here and we all know what comes next."

What comes next? What was he talking about? And then I remembered the track listings. The Doomsday Prophecies. What had Apocalips said again? Nothing can stop us? So what came after that?

Of course. "Who's the child with the voice of light?" I asked.

There were no smirks anymore. The four of them exchanged puzzled glances.

"You really haven't worked it out yet?" said an incredulous Donnie. "Your part in the prophecy?"

It had been my favorite track. It had connected with me in a way that the other songs hadn't. But that's all it had been to me – a decent song. Now, though, it took on a whole new significance. I tried to remember the lyrics:

A king and a queen of song,
Living a life where they don't belong.
Only their prince with the voice of light
Can stop the riders and the infinite night...

It seemed obvious to me now. The king and queen were my parents, living a life as accountants instead of singers. So this meant… "I'm the child with the voice of light? You mean it's my destiny to stop you destroying the world? How? By singing!?!"

"First of all," said Donnie, "please don't undersell this thing. We're not just going to destroy the world. We're going to destroy everything. Every world, every universe, every dimension. Gone in just a few hours. It's foretold in prophecies that have existed since the moment things started existing. And yes, you do get a mention. But don't get too excited, the prophecies are very clear on what *we* will accomplish but less so on what you're going to do."

Donnie began to pace the room, looking agitated for the first time. "We've spent several millennia reading the things," he went on, "and as far as we can tell, your chances of stopping us are about a hundred trillion billion to one. Even so, after waiting so long, we weren't going to risk it. That's why we came up with a plan to get you in the band."

To … get me in the band. What was going on here?

"The whole thing with Steve was set up for your benefit," said Pete. "We knew you were watching. We didn't kill him, we just sent him to another dimension for safekeeping. We could have just used a hotel room, I guess, but we didn't want to risk anyone hearing him. And plus, creating a portal to another dimension? Well, it's a laugh, isn't it?"

"We had to give you a reason to want to join us," continued Frankie. "So we set up a little light show in that storage room. We knew you'd take the bait."

"Keep your friends close, your enemies closer,

and your enemies who might somehow stop you destroying all of creation, keep them closest of all," said Donnie.

"You actually wanted me in the band?" I said.

"Of course we did," said Frankie. "How else do you think you made it through that audition so easily? You really thought it was your dancing? I mean, it wasn't *that* bad for a week's effort but come on."

Finally the audition process started to make sense. "So that's why you didn't want people singing? You're afraid of me? Of … of my voice, is that it?"

"We were," said Warren. "Until we found this."

He was holding up Milo's Sing-Sync device. I raised my hand to grab it, but Warren shoved me backward with no effort at all. He smiled before crushing the retainer in his massive fist.

"So it was you who took it from my bedroom," I said.

"Of course it was," said Frankie. "We knew something was up when you randomly stopped wearing it. So we had one of the housekeepers bring it to us."

"It's an impressive device," said Donnie. "The prophecies didn't bother mentioning that the voice of light wouldn't actually belong to you. I suppose you could argue that it's a technicality. Me, I'd say you were a fraud. Just like us. As the next track on the album says, we are 'Not Who We Say We Are.'"

"Then who are you?" I demanded. "Show me."

The band members seemed to find this funny. "Trust us, Sammy," said Donnie. "You wouldn't want to see us in our true form. It would shock you to the very core of your soul."

"Your puny little brain wouldn't be able to handle the horrors you would see before you," said Frankie.

"You would weep in our presence," said Pete.

"You would cower in fear," said Warren.

"Oh, be quiet," I said. "Just show me."

So they did.

And they were right. Their true forms were the most hideous sights I could ever have pictured.

"Surprise," said the figure that had been Donnie but was now Veronica Heatherstone.

APOCALIPS

CHAPTER TWENTY-FOUR

★★★

"You?" I said.

"Us!" said the Heatherstones.

"But … but…" I stammered.

"Hang on," said Steve, looking outraged. "You mean to tell me that all this time, I was actually in a girl band?"

"A demon band more like," I said, still scrambling to get my head around this.

"As our biggest threat, we've been monitoring you closely for years," said Veronica. "By infiltrating your class from primary school, we were able to learn a great deal about you."

"There was also the added bonus that we were able to make your life miserable for years," said Vicky, formerly Warren. The others nodded in agreement.

"We knew that in the run-up to Hyde Park we weren't going to have time to keep an eye on you ourselves," said Valerie, sweeping strands of hair out of her eyes, a leftover from her guise as Pete. "But our plans were too important to let you run around unchecked. We weren't sure what to do."

"But then something unexpected and wonderful happened," said Violet, formerly Frankie. "At school we overheard your sister's friend Amy talking about going to the Apocalips concert. She mentioned that you'd be there, too. That's when we came up with a plan to get you into the band. The first step was to shut you in that storage room so that you could witness our little performance piece."

"But … how could you have done that? You were onstage at the time."

Valerie thumbed toward Steve. "Actually, it was just him onstage. We let him do one of his boring solos while we took care of you."

"Hey, you all said you liked them," said a hurt-looking Steve.

"What about at the start of the concert?" I said. "You were right in front of us when Apocalips – or you, I guess – came out onstage."

"You mean when the lights went out?" said Veronica, standing in front of me one second, then clicking her fingers and appearing behind me the next. "We have powers you couldn't even begin to imagine."

"So you were in on this?" I said to Steve.

"What, no!" said Steve. "Well, all right, some of it I knew. I was fine with the acting stuff, pretending I was ready to quit the band. I've got aspirations to take up acting once I'm done with the music industry so this was a good chance for me to hone my skills." Steve waved his hands theatrically as he said the word acting.

"I wasn't aware I'd be imprisoned in another dimension," he went on. "I didn't realize that they really do want to destroy everything, and I had no idea that they were actually girls. If I'd known about all that … well … I'd have probably talked it over with my agent at least."

There were still bits that didn't make sense. "If you're so powerful, why go to all this trouble?" I said, turning back to the Heatherstones. "Why can't you just use your powers to destroy everything yourselves? And if I'm such a threat, why not just kill me years ago?"

"Sadly our powers are not yet great enough for

that," said Veronica. "But soon that will change. Very soon, in fact."

"Ooh, maybe they can't kill you!" chipped in Steve.

The Heatherstones looked mildly embarrassed.

"That's er … correct…" said Valerie. "We are forbidden by the ancient laws of the multiverse to directly kill a living soul."

"Which is totally unfair," pouted Vicky.

"Rest assured that no law made by man, woman or supernatural being will be enough to stop our destiny from being realized," insisted Veronica.

"OK then, why didn't you just banish me here when I was a baby or something?"

"Because prophecies have a habit of coming true once you take your eye off them. It was important for us to keep you close. Only once we had learned all we possibly could about you, could we be sure that you no longer posed a threat. And since we've learned that you're not much more than a lip-syncing cheat, I think that time has come.

Our time has come."

The Heatherstones' eyes suddenly turned dark and glassy, like Lexi's had when she was under their control. "For we are the Four Horsewomen of the Apocalypse," they boomed. "The end of days is upon us. Death and destruction will rain down as we take our final ride."

Veronica extended her hand. "Join us, for our final performance. There must be five. It is the Universal Law of Boy Bands."

I almost laughed in her face. "You've got to be kidding, right?" I said. "I'll never join you."

"She wasn't speaking to you, halfwit," said Violet.

Steve reached out and took Veronica's hand.

"Are you crazy?" I shouted. "They're going to destroy everything. Is that what you want?"

Steve looked back at me. "Of course it isn't," he said solemnly. "But it's pretty obvious that nothing is going to stop them. So my choice is to spend my last moments stuck in some cave or out there onstage in front of all my fans. At least I can make their last moments on earth enjoyable ones."

"How noble," said Veronica. She picked up a remote control that was lying on the end of the bed and tossed it toward me. "We'd hate for you of all people to miss the spectacle. You can watch it on TV. So long, Sammy. I can honestly say that we'll all miss making your life miserable."

The glowing door reappeared, and I watched in disbelief as the five of them walked back through it. I raced after them, but just as I got there the portal vanished, leaving me alone with nothing but the echoes of the Heatherstones' laughter ringing in my ears.

CHAPTER TWENTY-FIVE

★★★

I had failed everyone. My whole life I'd wanted to be special in some way, and then I find out that I might be the only person who can stop the Apocalypse. As talents go, that has to be quite high on the list, right? Definitely higher than being able to touch your nose with your tongue, for example. But instead of saving the world, I end up stuck inside a hotel room in another dimension.

Typical. Well, not typical … but you know what I mean.

I spent ages searching for a way out of the room, but there wasn't so much as a single crack in the cave walls. I had no idea how air was even getting into this place, but after taking a bottle of cola out of the fridge and watching a new bottle materialize in its place, I stopped worrying about logic.

Out of ideas, I switched on the TV to watch the coverage of the Apocalypse. I didn't have to look far. The concert was being shown live on every channel.

"We're here at Hyde Park where all the talk is about the secret finale," said a reporter, dressed for the occasion in denim shorts, a pair of green boots and a cowboy hat. "Spokespeople for the band remain tight-lipped but have assured us that it's going to be unlike anything ever seen before…"

It seemed safe to say that the end of the world would definitely be that.

Then the news leaked. Steve was back with the band, and I was out. Pretty much everyone seemed to agree that this was a good thing. Even under the circumstances I couldn't help but feel a little offended. Steve and I both had our pros and cons and no one seemed to be appreciating that.

	Steve	Me
Strong Singer	✓	✗
Strong Dancer	✓	✗
Striking Haircut	✓	✗
Stage Presence	✓	✗
Willing to bring about the Apocalypse	✓	✗

Maybe it's just me, but I definitely think the last one was more important than which of us could sing a cheesy ballad the best.

My phone rang. I took it out of my pocket and stared at it in disbelief. I hadn't even considered using it, being in another dimension and everything. But had I not been trapped in enough places by the Heatherstones by now to always check the simplest things first? I mean, seriously.

"Milo?" I said, pressing the answer button.

"Sam… Thank goodness you're still alive. Where are you? What's happened?"

"Well, the good news is that I got inside that room on the 28th floor," I said. "The bad news is that I'm now trapped in a cave in another dimension. With really good phone and TV reception apparently."

"It's all over the news that Steve is back," said Milo. "Wait … did you just say you're in another dimension?"

"Yeah… I can explain everything later, but you have to get me out of here," I said. "You don't happen to know anything about inter-dimensional portals by any chance, do you?"

"No, not really," admitted Milo. "I mean obviously I'm familiar with the many worlds interpretation of quantum mechanics and the fundamental concepts of traversable wormholes, but who isn't these days, right? It's all theoretical stuff, though. It could take me years to figure out a practical use for any of it."

"Right," I said, not understanding a word of what he had just said. "Well, do you think you can come over here and try opening the door?"

There was a pause on the other end. "Opening the door?"

"Yeah, the door on the 28th floor," I said. "I think it only works one way for humans. Steve and I couldn't get out, but the Heatherstones could."

"The Heatherstones?" shouted Milo, almost deafening me in the process.

"I'll tell you everything when you get here. Just hurry," I said.

"All right," said Milo. "Stay where you are, I'm coming to get you."

Stay where I am? I thought as he ended the call. Where exactly was I going to go?

I waited helplessly in the cave, jumping between TV channels building up to the concert. Not a single one had any idea what was coming. It was almost five o'clock now, which meant it was only minutes until the concert began. I was starting to think that I really was going to have to sit back and watch the end of the world on live TV when Milo and Lexi burst into the room. "Sam!" they said, throwing their arms around me.

My excitement at seeing them again vanished seconds later when I heard the sound of a door slamming shut. The three of us looked back at the spot where moments before had been a glowing portal back to earth and where there now was just a cave wall.

My mouth opened and shut a few times. There were no words.

Just as I was about to drop to my knees and start crying, the portal reappeared, and two figures I hadn't seen in a long time stepped part of the way in.

"Mom, Dad!" I shouted.

APOCALIPS

CHAPTER TWENTY-SIX

★★★

"Bit of a spring on that door, isn't there?" remarked Mom, holding it open. She turned to Milo and Lexi. "Good job we're not as fast as you two or we might all have ended up stuck in here."

"Still, probably best if we get a move on," suggested Dad.

The three of us didn't need any convincing as we hurried through the portal and back into the corridor of the 28th floor. I threw my arms around my parents, hugging them like I had never voluntarily hugged them before.

"Oh, I'm so glad to see you, Sam," said Mom.

"We both are," said Dad. "And after discussing it, your mother and I think it best if you knock this boy band business on the head. On account of them being supernatural beings intent on destroying the universe and all."

I blinked a few times, unable to quite grasp what I had just heard. "So … you believe me now about Apocalips?"

"Of course we do," said Dad. "As soon as Milo explained it to us we came straight to get you."

I stared at them in disbelief. "So you believed Milo as soon as he told you?"

"Well… Yes, sweetheart," said Mom. "It's Milo we're talking about after all. I mean the boy wouldn't say boo to a goose, but he's so smart that if he told me I could get rich by eating my own boogers, I'd believe him."

"Um … thanks," said Milo, clearly unsure about just how much of a compliment that was. "And you can't. Get rich from eating your own boogers, I mean. Not that I'm aware of, anyway."

"Noted," said Mom, tapping her forehead.

"Why didn't you believe *me* when I told you?" I said.

"Oh … well," said Mom. "Help me out here, Harold."

"We … we're sorry, son," said Dad.

"We are, Sam," said Mom. "Can you forgive us?"

It would have been nice to have been annoyed at them for a little while, but there wasn't time. There was an apocalypse to avert. "Fine, I forgive you," I said. "Now we need to get over to Hyde Park."

"*Hyde Park?*" said Mom, looking at me as if I had just suggested she punch me in the face.

"We're not going anywhere near that place," said Dad. "We're getting in the car and driving as far away from there as possible. We'll have to pick Milo's mom up first so it might get a bit tight in the back, but we should manage."

"NO!" I said. "Don't you get it? It's the Apocalypse. We can't outrun it."

My parents exchanged worried looks. "Sam,

if that's the case then what can we possibly do?" asked Mom.

The truth was I had no idea. But I told them everything I knew. About Apocalips being the Heatherstones and about the Heatherstones being the Four Horsewomen of the Apocalypse. About the prophecies. And about their son being the child with the voice of light – the only one who could stop the Horsewomen.

"I can't believe the Heatherstones are actually demons," put in Milo.

Lexi shot him a puzzled look. "Really?"

"Actually, you're right, it does explain a lot about them," he said.

"So you see," I said, "I'm the only chance we have of stopping them. You have to get me to the concert."

"He's right, Martha," said Dad. "We can't just keep running away from things."

Mom closed her eyes and nodded. "I know. Although, Sam... I have to say ... about this child with the voice of light..."

"Yes?" I said, getting a little annoyed that no one was moving yet.

"Well, son, it's just… Don't you think…?" said Dad, squirming a little. "How can I put this?"

Lexi threw her hands up in the air. "For crying out loud, Sam. The prophecy is obviously about Milo, not you."

"What?" said Milo.

"What?" I repeated. "What are you talking about? Have you even heard the lyrics?"

"Yeah, they released the album this morning," said Lexi.

"Well, then, you know it goes," I said, trying to remember the words.

"A king and a queen of song,
Living a life where they don't belong.
Only their prince with the voice of light
Can stop the riders and the infinite night…
…something something…
…if the song rings out, if the song rings true
Then the plans of those riders may yet fall through…"

I turned to Mom and Dad. "The king and queen … that's you guys."

They blushed a little.

"And their prince," I continued. "Well, that's their son, obviously. *With the voice of light*. It has to be me."

"Actually, Sam," said Milo, his voice almost a whisper. "It doesn't actually say that the voice is yours."

What was happening here?

"Yes, it does," I said. "*The prince with the voice of light*."

Why was no else getting this?

"But it was my voice singing at the audition," said Milo. "What if the prophecy means you, as the prince, along *with* me as the voice of light?"

"Because no offense, Sam," said Lexi, which obviously meant she was about to say something offensive. "Your singing is horrible. A voice of light is going to at least be in tune, isn't it?"

I opened my mouth to argue, then realized that they were probably right. Maybe the Heatherstones had misunderstood the prophecy, just like I had. And I had to admit, Donnie/Veronica did have a point. There was still a part of me that wanted to be special. I had started to think that I was going to get to be like those characters in books that turn out to have amazing talent. But I had to accept that those were fantasy stories and this was real, and it was bigger than me or anyone else. It didn't matter that I wasn't the child with the voice of light, what mattered was stopping the end of the world.

"Right," I said, swallowing my pride. "Then *we* need to get to Hyde Park. Now."

Without any more arguments, we piled into the elevator. We remained on our guard for anyone getting in, but no one did. I had a feeling everyone from the building would be at the concert. On the way down, lots of little bits of information I had learned in the last few weeks began to jump around in my head. Moments that I didn't really understand at the time now started to make sense, and things that had seemed unimportant now felt like they might be the key to everything. If I didn't know any better, it was almost like my brain was starting to come up with a plan.

By the time the doors opened on the ground floor, I had it. I couldn't help but smile as we got into the car. Milo turned to me.

"You've got something, haven't you?" he asked.

"I think so…" I said. "But you're not going to like it."

"Why?"

"Because there's a chance you're going to have to sing," I said. "In front of two hundred thousand people."

Milo's face turned green. "I think I'm going to throw up."

APOCALIPS

CHAPTER TWENTY-SEVEN

★ ★ ★

Fortunately Milo didn't throw up, but it was touch and go for most of the way. I managed to make him feel slightly better after explaining my plan to him. If things went as I hoped, then there was still the chance he might not have to sing at all.

While trying to stop Milo from spewing his guts out was a problem, it wasn't our biggest one. The closer we were getting to Hyde Park, the slower we were moving, until eventually traffic came to a complete stop. We were still at least a couple of miles away.

"Looks like they've shut off all the roads near

the park," said Dad.

"Come on," I said. "We'll have to go on foot."

We abandoned the car and started running toward the park. Half an hour later, breathless and sweating, we finally arrived at the entrance.

"These four are with me," I said to the ticket checker, who looked startled when she recognized me. Even if she hadn't, we were surrounded by posters that still had my face plastered on them, so the "Don't you know who I am" card would have been an easy one to play. But without saying a word she waved us all through.

We were pretty far from the stage, but thanks to the giant screens placed throughout the park we could see the Heatherstones or Apocalips or the Horsewomen or whatever you wanted to call them performing the song "Baby." They were about halfway through. Or at least I thought they were. It's quite hard to know with a song that basically only has one word. But I did know from having seen the set list that we were already pretty far into the concert.

"What's that blue stuff?" asked Milo, pointing just above the crowd. It took me a second or two to see it. The hundreds of thousands of screaming fans appeared to be generating a faint blue mist. It seemed to rise a few feet above the crowd before drifting toward the stage. Toward the band.

"'*They are what give us strength. We feed off their love*,'" I said.

"What?" asked Lexi.

"That's what Donnie … I mean, Veronica, used to say about the fans in interviews," I said. "Now I'm thinking she didn't mean it in some wishy-washy way, she meant literally. They're feeding off the love of the fans. They're drawing strength off two hundred thousand people screaming their heads off. And when do you think the screams will be the loudest?"

"At the finale," said Milo.

The answer had been right in front of me the entire time. The energy that had passed through me standing on the balcony after the audition had been overwhelming, but that had been nothing compared to what was happening now. With that amount of power in the hands of the Horsewomen, the Apocalypse suddenly seemed quite possible.

"What's the plan?" asked Dad.

Just beyond him I noticed a chain-link fence separating the fans from the backstage area. "OK, Lexi and Milo, I need you both to come with me,"

I said, pointing toward the fence. "We need to get backstage."

"How are we going to do that?" asked Milo.

"Leave it to me," I said.

"Sam, what can we do?" asked Mom.

I looked out at the crowd. Just by being there and adoring their beloved band, the Apocalytes were helping the Horsewomen. "Try and get as many people as you can to go home," I said.

"How?" asked Dad.

"I don't know, figure it out," I said.

"Be careful," said Dad.

"We love you," said Mom.

"Love you, too," I said, turning away and trying not to think about the fact that it might be the last time we'd ever see each other.

APOCALIPS

CHAPTER TWENTY-EIGHT

★★★

"Where do you think you're going? Oh … it's you."

The path to the backstage area was blocked by a security guard. It took me a couple of seconds to remember that it was the one who had greeted me when I first arrived at the audition. Well, "greeted" was probably stretching it, but he had been there at least.

"Hello, Brian," I said.

"Remember me, do you?" asked Brian. "Well, I must say I didn't think I'd ever see you again."

I couldn't help frowning a little. "Yeah, you didn't think I would win, did you?"

Brian looked a little lost at this. "Oh, you mean the competition? Oh no, I definitely didn't think you'd win. I thought you were an AHNT if ever I saw one."

"An ant?" I asked.

Brian sighed. "No, not an ant – an AHNT. A. H. N. T. Stands for: All Haircut, No Talent."

"Oh," I said. Well, Brian had been correct there.

"But obviously I was wrong," said Brian.

"Er ... yeah, obviously," I said.

"Then again, maybe not," said Brian. "Since you're clearly not in the band anymore. That's what I meant by not expecting to see you again."

"Sorry?" I said, forcing a laugh. I looked around at Milo and Lexi who added to the laughter, despite clearly having no idea where I was going with this. "Who told you that I wasn't in the band anymore? Of course I'm still in the band."

"Sure you are," said Brian. "That's why you're here, and the rest of the band are up there. Wait ... why are you here?"

"Because I'm still in the band, Brian," I said. "When Steve wanted to come back Nigel decided that we'd continue as a six-piece."

"A six-member boy band?" Brian scratched his head. "That doesn't sound very likely."

"Yeah, well, Nigel wants to try something new," I said. "Anyway, I was supposed to play the whole thing, but then Nigel felt that performing in the biggest show the world has ever known was asking a lot of a first-timer. You can understand that, right?"

"Hmm… I guess—"

"Exactly," I interrupted. "So Nigel thought it would be better if Steve did the show, and I came out as a surprise for the final song. Makes sense, huh?"

"Well, I suppose… But…"

"Think about it," I said. "If I wasn't in the band, I'd hardly be here right now trying to get backstage, would I? And with my friends… I mean, my entourage." Ignoring the looks I was getting from Lexi and Milo, I pressed on. "I'd be far too busy moping about how I lost my one and only shot at fame, wouldn't I?"

Brian stroked his chin a few times as he pondered what I'd said. Eventually he just shrugged. "Yeah, I suppose that does make sense. So you're still in the band then? Pfft. I shouldn't be surprised. Nobody tells me anything around here. But how come you're just turning up now? The concert's almost over."

Without missing a beat I smiled and said, "Slept in."

Brian looked at his watch. "It's half-past six."

"Yeah, but I am a celebrity."

Brian rolled his eyes. "You all live on a different planet. All right, in you go."

No one paid us any attention as we made our way through the backstage area. Everyone was far too busy to notice three kids slipping in among them, even when, until a few hours ago, one of those kids had been scheduled to be one of the stars onstage.

Eventually we found what I was looking for –

the production truck. I pushed open the door, and the three of us stepped into the back. It was dark inside, except for the light coming from the banks of monitors.

"Hey, what are you doing here?" From the shadows emerged an angry-looking man. He had a thick, bristly beard that he seemed to be using to store his lunch in. Around his neck hung a pair of headphones.

"Are you the tech guy?" I asked.

"No, I'm just lost," said the man in a sarcastic voice. "I don't know what any of these buttons do."

The man stared at us for a few seconds before letting out a long, exaggerated sigh. "Of course I'm the tech guy," he said. "What else would I be doing in the tech truck? Seriously, though, you kids need to get out of here, the finale's coming up in a minute. And it's not worth my life if that gets messed up."

Funny he should say that, I thought.

"Er … Nigel sent us," I said. "He's got a last-minute change he needs for the final song."

"Oh, really," said the tech guy, taking a phone out of his pocket. "Well, why don't I speak to Nigel himself and find out."

As he began looking through his contacts, the tech guy failed to notice the ten-year-old girl sneaking up behind him or the sack that she removed from the inside pocket of her jacket. It was over in a flash. Lexi tied the drawstring with the grace and speed of a ninja. The tech guy's phone clattered to the ground.

"Consider yourself sacked," said Lexi triumphantly.

"So you just carry one of those everywhere you go now, do you?" I asked Lexi as the security guard wriggled around on the ground muttering words that it's probably best I don't repeat.

"What can I say, they do keep coming in handy," she said. "Well, what's the plan? We switch off all the power, stop the show?"

I shook my head. The thought of sabotaging the show had occurred to me, but it would only be a temporary fix. Nigel Cruul would have people here fixing the problem within seconds. We'd buy the world fifteen to twenty minutes' more time at most. No, hopefully there was a longer-lasting solution.

As I took out my phone and handed it to Milo, I explained my plan. Milo nodded and got to work. After a quick check of the tech guy's workstation, he found a cable and managed to connect the phone to the system. He spent the next few minutes tapping commands into a keyboard.

"Hey, you'd better not be touching my console,"

shouted the tech guy. "Is that typing? I can hear typing."

"Shh, you," said Lexi.

There wasn't much for Lexi and me to do but stand around waiting.

"So," said Lexi. "We're your entourage now?"

I smiled. "No. You guys have *always* been my entourage."

"Seriously, though," she said, "that was some high-quality lying back there."

"Thanks," I said, wondering if I might have finally found my hidden talent after all. Then a thought occurred to me. "Hey, Lexi?"

"What?" she said.

"Do you ... you know?"

"What?"

"Want a hug?"

Lexi looked at me with horror. "Why?" she asked.

"Well ... because you're my sister... And the world might be coming to an end."

Lexi considered this. "Do you?"

I thought about it. "I don't know. Maybe?"

"Right," said Lexi.

"So what do you think?" I asked.

"I don't know," she said. "I guess…"

"Oh, for crying out loud, just give each other a hug," said the tech guy, his voice muffled through the sack.

"Shh," we said together.

"Right, that's it, I'm done," said Milo.

"Phew," said Lexi.

"One problem," said Milo. "The system won't let it play with the current track, so I've had to cue it up. It should hit when the last track comes on, which will be in two minutes and … five seconds. If I've done it right, that is."

"Well, let's go and find out," I said.

"Hey, you're not just going to leave me tied up here, are you?" said the tech guy.

"No, we're definitely going to come back and untie you," said Lexi.

"Great," said the tech guy. "Hey, wait, was that

sarcasm? Hello? Hello?"

We bolted out of the door and headed toward the stage. We were almost at the steps leading onto it when we ran straight into Nigel Cruul.

APOCALIPS

CHAPTER TWENTY-NINE

★★★

"What are *you* doing here?" snapped Cruul, looking me up and down like something he'd have someone else remove from his shoe.

"Trying to stop the Apocalypse," I said.

Cruul didn't laugh or look shocked at this. He simply rolled his eyes. "You can't stop it. No one can."

"So you know?" I asked.

"Of course I do," he said coolly.

"Well, we have to try," I said. "Help us."

"Help you?" he said, looking bemused. "Now why would I do that?"

I glanced around at the others, wondering if it

was a trick question.

"Because the Apocalypse would be … bad," said Milo.

"Maybe in your eyes, but not mine," said Cruul.

"You're wasting your time, Sam," said Lexi. "He's obviously under their spell."

Cruul let out a derisive little laugh. "I most certainly am not," he said. "With me there was no need. I was more than happy to go along with their plans."

I couldn't believe it. "You willingly helped the Four Horsewomen of the Apocalypse?"

"After what they offered me? Of course," said Cruul. "My career was in ruins when I met them. I had an act – a pop duo. They were huge, on the cusp of greatness. Then they quit on me just before I could take them to the next level. I spent years trying to claw my way back, with nothing but failure after failure. Then one night, at my lowest point, they came to me in my studio – these four identical girls who could change their form at will.

They offered me a chance to become the biggest, most successful music promoter of all time. They would use their powers and influence to rebuild my career. Once I became the most powerful figure in the industry I could then help create the greatest boy band of all time. We would shatter all records, make more money than anyone, and then my legacy would be cemented for all time. No one would ever be more successful than Nigel Cruul."

"Because everyone would be dead!" I shouted.

Nigel shrugged. "That, my boy, is the price of fame. And it's about to be paid."

"I wouldn't be so sure," said Milo, pointing toward the stage.

As the opening bars of "The Last Ride" rang out across the park, the five members of Apocalips took their positions, waiting for the vocals to start. But no one was really watching them. Everyone was too busy gazing up at the video clip that was playing on the giant screens.

It started with a close-up of a door. Four

handsome young men, better known to the world as Donnie, Warren, Frankie and Pete entered the room. Then the time stamp on the video started to speed up, skipping ahead to almost ten minutes later, when Steve and four identical blond girls, looking very pleased with themselves, left the room.

"What is this?" said Nigel Cruul.

"It's video footage from the security camera on the 28th floor," said Milo. "It was Sam's idea. I just made a few edits."

"I'll never forget the first lesson I ever learned from you, Nigel," I said, leaning in. "No girlfriends."

"But those aren't their girlfriends," said a flustered Cruul. "I mean, that's them, that's Apocalips."

"Yeah, we know that," I said. I pointed toward the crowd. "But *they* don't. And it's the *appearance* of availability that's important, remember."

The effect was instantaneous. Large pockets of the crowd had already begun to leave as Apocalips, continuing with their Simulated Vocal Performance™, found themselves being drowned out by booing on an industrial scale. The blue mist was flowing away from the stage.

"You idiots, what have you done?" said Cruul. "You've ruined everything."

Cruul looked like he was about to have a meltdown. He turned with a wild look in his eyes and lunged toward me. Lexi reached out to grab him, but he was too quick. As I tried to run, I lost my footing and tumbled to the ground. Just as Cruul was about to land on top of me, there was a thud and he went flying backward.

I looked up to see Mom, shaking her right fist at a cowering Cruul. Dad grabbed her arm, holding her back.

"Leave it, Martha," said Dad. "He's not worth it."

"I should have done that to him back when he was our manager," she said.

"Honestly, you wonder where Lexi gets it from," sighed Dad.

I realized that now probably wasn't the time to ask questions. Milo and Lexi helped me to my feet, and together the five of us ran over to the side of the stage.

"We managed to get a few people out," said Mom. "Your dad and I pretended to be security guards who needed to evacuate the park. We were doing quite well, until the real security guards turned up, and we had to run for it. Looks like you've done the job though, Sam."

Up onstage Apocalips were busy calling for their former fans to stay put.

"Come back," shouted Donnie in desperation. "It's not what you think. Those aren't our girlfriends. Look!"

Apocalips, with the exception of Steve, transformed into the Heatherstones.

Unsurprisingly, it didn't help their cause. On the plus side, the boos stopped, but the screams that replaced them were arguably even louder, despite the fact that a third of the crowd had already left. And these were not the **I-LOVE-YOU** screams the band was used to. These were more **OH-I'VE-NEVER-BEEN-SO-FRIGHTENED** screams.

"I think that's just made it worse," noted Steve.

"Be quiet," yelled an enraged Vicky.

"Why don't you be quiet?"

The voice that spoke didn't have a mic, but it was still loud enough to be heard over the noise. It was Lexi. She had that look in her eye. The look she always has just before a fight's about to go down.

APOCALIPS

CHAPTER THIRTY

★★★

"Lexi, no," I shouted. But it was too late. She charged across the stage.

"Get her," screamed Veronica.

I peered through my fingers as Lexi dived through the air, wiping out Violet with a flying body splash. She rolled straight through, grabbing Valerie by the ankles and tripping her. Lexi sprang to her feet just as Veronica lunged at her with a punch, then ducked, grabbing the Horsewoman by the waist. She flipped Veronica several feet into the air, right into the path of Violet, who had only just made it back to her feet. The two of them crashed to the ground in a heap,

right in front of a terrified-looking Steve. Then it was
Lexi vs. Vicky. There was a brief stare down before
Vicky charged toward her, launching herself into
a flying kick. Lexi rolled out of the way at the last
second. But she hadn't seen Valerie, who grabbed
her from behind, pinning back her arms. Seeing her
opportunity, Vicky raced toward them. Her arms still
behind her, Lexi threw her legs into the air, wrapping
them around Vicky's head. With a twist of her body
she sent Vicky's head on a collision course with
Valerie's identical one.

As the Heatherstones writhed around on the ground in agony, Lexi couldn't resist giving a little bow to the crowd, who were eating it all up, whooping and hollering in support.

But as I looked out at the crowd, I gave a gasp of horror. The blue mist was rising again, flowing toward the Heatherstones faster than ever.

They were feeding off everyone's enjoyment at seeing four older girls losing a fight to a ten-year-old.

"Lexi, stop!" I screamed, but it was too late.

The Heatherstones rose to their feet, exchanging knowing smiles.

"I told you there were better ways to extract joy than by being a boy band," laughed Valerie. "Humans have always loved a good fight."

"Yeah, we should have been pro wrestlers," said Vicky.

"It's done now," said Veronica. "It's time for the Horsewomen to ride."

From the darkness of the stage behind them emerged the four huge horses I had seen in rehearsals.

Red, black, white and the palest of greens, somehow they looked even less real and even more intimidating than before. If you could make animals from fear and hatred alone, then those four horses would probably be what you'd end up with.

Polly the pony trotted nervously out behind them. I should have known Cruul wouldn't get me a replacement horse.

The Heatherstones mounted their steeds, and Steve reluctantly mounted Polly. Suddenly the Heatherstones galloped toward the edge of the stage before leaping into the air. But rather than landing in the crowd, they rose above it and began circling the park at a thunderous speed.

Steve looked down at Polly, who tossed her mane as if to say "Forget it."

As the horses raced across the sky, they left trails of smoke in their wake, creating a huge spiraling column. The sky began to darken, day quickly becoming night. There was a crack that sounded like thunder, but it was no storm. It was the sound of the sky itself ripping.

"What's happening?" cried Lexi, rushing back toward us.

"They're tearing the world apart," I said. I turned to Milo. "It's time."

Milo was shaking. "I can't," he whispered.

"Yes, you can," I said. "You have to."

Milo looked out at the stage, then toward the sky, then back to me.

"Even if it goes wrong," I said, trying to sound reassuring, "I can guarantee no one will make fun of you over it."

"Because we'll all be dead," said Lexi.

"You can do it, Milo," said Mom.

"We believe in you," said Dad.

Just when it seemed like Milo was about to throw up, his face turning a distinct shade of green, he didn't. As I looked into his eyes something seemed to spark within them. He gave me a nod, then ran onto the stage, grabbing a mic from one of the abandoned stands.

He sang the same song he had sung for me at

the audition, "Summer Funk." The upbeat lyrics, belted out across the park without any backing track, gave the imminent Apocalypse an extra layer of bizarreness. And Milo didn't just sing the song, he danced too, owning the stage as if he had been born to it.

He was sensational.

But Milo's performance made no difference at all. The tear in the sky was getting bigger by the second.

APOCALIPS

CHAPTER THIRTY-ONE

★★★

"It's not working," shouted Milo as the all-too-familiar sound of Heatherstone laughter echoed from above.

"I don't understand," said Mom. "What about the prophecy?"

"Who else could it be?" said Dad.

I ran across the stage, grabbing hold of Milo.

"Come on," I shouted. "We need to get out of here."

But Milo didn't move. He turned to me and handed me the microphone. "Then it must be you."

"What?" I said. "But how? I can't sing, remember?"

Milo didn't seem to have the answer, either. He stared up at the dark sky, then after a moment something seemed to dawn on his face. "Of course!" he shouted, throwing his hands in the air. "It's so obvious."

"It's *really* not," I said.

"But it is," he said, excitedly pointing to the sky. "It's Newton's third law."

"Which one's that again?" I asked.

"The one about every action having an equal and opposite reaction," he said. "What's the opposite of darkness?"

"Light?" I said, unsure where this was heading.

"Exactly," said Milo. "Now think about this: the Horsewomen managed to create darkness from people's joy and adoration. But if light is the opposite of darkness then that means that the voice of light would have to be one that—"

"Filled people with despair?" I said. "Hang on, you're telling me that the only way to stop them is for me to sing my worst?"

Milo nodded. "Your *absolute* worst," he said. "You're going to have to give the worst performance of your life."

I remembered back to the last time I had sung in public. The time my parents took Lexi and me caroling. I hadn't wanted to go, I remember thinking it was silly. Knowing about my parents' past, it made sense to me now why they had taken us. They had just wanted to sing in front of people again. We had barely made it to the chorus of "Jingle Bells" when that idea came crashing down, thanks to my horrible voice. The grimaces on our neighbors' faces, the hands clamping over their ears, the doors slamming shut – it all came back to me.

I looked up at the sky and smiled.

"Dashing through the snow, in a one-horse open sleigh..."

"You're going with 'Jingle Bells'?" said Milo, covering his ears. "In June?"

No, I thought. *I'm murdering "Jingle Bells" in June.*

"O'er the fields we go, laughing all the way."

I made no attempt to stay in key. I hit all the wrong notes. It was a spectacular failure and a glorious success at the same time. Every word that left my lips was a brutal assault on the ears. It was probably 50/50 as to whether the crowd was fleeing because of the end of the world or because of my performance.

"Bells on bobtail ring, making spirits bright, what fun it is to ride and sing, a sleighing song tonight."

As badly as the crowd was taking it – many fans had given up fleeing altogether and just dropped to the ground, covering their ears – it wasn't going down particularly well above me, either. There was no longer any laughter coming from the Horsewomen as they realized that the hole was starting to shrink. Light was beginning to pierce through the sky above, like bullet holes.

It was working.

"Jingle bells, jingle bells, jingle all the way. Oh what fun it is to ride in a one-horse open sleigh."

As I began repeating the chorus, I looked up at the sky. The rip had almost mended itself, the hole now only a few feet wide. The Horsewomen were in disarray, no longer able to control their mounts. As otherworldly as the horses appeared to be, even they knew when it was time to bolt. But as they twisted and bucked in the sky, it became clear that the smoke trails were now more like tendrils, winding around the horses and dragging them toward the hole. There was genuine fear now on the faces of the Horsewomen. It was a look I had never seen on any of the Heatherstones before.

Several of the tendrils yanked back suddenly, and Violet was gone, tumbling helplessly into the swirling abyss. Seconds later the same thing happened to Valerie. True to form, Vicky wasn't going down without a fight, screaming at her demon horse to gallop away from the hole. It made little difference, buying her a few more seconds until she, too, vanished.

I looked around for Veronica, but there was no sign of her. Just when I had assumed she must have slipped silently into the void, I heard her booming voice.

"**NOOOO!**" she screamed. "The Four Horsewomen of the Apocalypse will not be defeated by a mere boy. Especially not one as annoying as you. I will not allow it. I might not be able to kill you, but I'll bring you to a place that will make you wish I could."

At that Veronica dived toward me, a single hand on the reins of her pale-green horse and the other reaching out toward me. The smoke tendrils were wrapping around her. Soon they would retract and pull her and her horse into the void. But not before she reached me and took me with her. I broke into a sprint, but it was no good, she was moving too fast. Wherever it was the Horsewomen were going, I was going, too.

Then, as Veronica's cold hand was about to reach me, I heard a whinny behind me, then a great weight slammed into my back. I flew across the stage, landing in a crumpled heap. I turned over just in time to see a confused-looking Veronica grabbing hold of a defiant-looking Steve riding an even more defiant-looking Polly.

Steve gave me a solemn nod. Then the remaining two Apocalips members, horse and pony included, were gone, and the hole along with them.

"Oh what fun it is to ride in a one-horse open sleigh," I sang to myself.

APOCALIPS

THE ENCORE

THREE MONTHS LATER

★ ★ ★

"Hey, where do you think you're going?"

I looked up at Brian the security guard. When he realized it was me, his face broke into a huge grin. "I'm so sorry, Sam," he said, lifting the red velvet rope and ushering me through. "They're all waiting for you."

"Thanks, Brian," I said.

I followed the low hum of laughter all the way along the corridor until I came to a room with a door that was slightly ajar. I pushed it open.

"Sam!"

"Sam the man," said Mickey, slapping me on the

back. "Glad you could make it."

"Of course," I said. "Thanks for inviting me."

"Are you kidding?" said Mickey. "You don't need an invitation. We wouldn't be here without you. Well, obviously, none of us would be here without you but I mean *here*, in this band."

"He's got a point," said Dad. "It was your idea to bring us together, after all."

Once all the fuss after the concert had died down a bit, it had occurred to me that with Apocalips retired, for want of a better word, there had been a pretty big gap left in the boy band market. And I thought I might just know the people to help fill it.

There was Mickey, of course. Even though everyone seemed to agree that I had pretty good reasons for doing so, I still felt like I owed him for cheating at the audition.

There was also Andy. That was the name of the boy Cruul and the others had mocked at the audition. I had tried and failed to stick up for him. Mickey had predicted that someone would give Andy a shot, but I'd never have imagined that person would turn out to be me.

"Thanks again," said Andy, giving me a fist bump.

Next was Barney, the boy who had known everything about stools. Barney was something of a boy band historian and, as it turned out, a great singer as well.

He looked up briefly from what appeared to be a boy band encyclopedia and gave me a nod.

"Sam, did you read that article I sent you about medieval boy bands?" he asked.

"No, not yet, but I'll definitely get around to it soon," I said. Lexi was right, I really did have a talent for lying.

"Hey, Sam, good to see you," came a voice from behind me.

"You too, Ritchie," I said, turning around. Ritchie, or Annoyed Boy as I once knew him, was a suggestion that I managed to surprise even myself with. But after Hyde Park I just couldn't stop thinking about Steve and how he had saved me at the end. People can always surprise you. Maybe it sounds silly, but it felt important to be able to give someone a second chance.

Luckily it seemed to pay off. Ritchie turned out to be a completely different person than the boy I first met at the audition. The almost Apocalypse seemed to have had that effect on a lot of people.

One in particular. He was smiling at me from across the room. The fifth and final member. Because a boy band should always have five members. Everyone knows that.

"You ready?" I asked him.

"As I'll ever be," said Milo.

"You'll be great," I said. "I think I saw your mom in the front row."

Milo's face went white. "Why did you tell me that?" he groaned. "I think I'm going to throw up. I mean it this time."

"Oh, Milo, relax," said my mom. "Sam, stop scaring our lead singer."

The band was called Aftermath. It seemed like an appropriate choice, and Milo really liked the fact that it had the word "math" in it.

Of course every band needs a good manager, and I had found two of them. I knew after everything that had happened, there was no way my parents could go back to being accountants. Who better to take Aftermath to the top than two people who had already been there? Even though they weren't performing themselves, I had never known my parents to be so happy. Needless to say their management style was worlds apart from Nigel Cruul's.

"Your sister phoned," said Dad. "She's not going to make it till a bit later. Practice has run on."

I had suggested to Lexi that she also try to find an outlet for her … er … talents. So she had taken up martial arts, signing up for classes in judo, karate and tae kwon do. Each of her instructors couldn't stop raving about how brilliant she was. They were all looking to train her for the Olympics. In fact a couple of weeks ago a fight had broken out between the three of them as they argued about which sport she was going to focus on. Luckily Lexi was nearby to break it up.

"All right, guys, it's showtime," said Mom.

As the band made their way to the stage, I walked behind them, just in case Milo tried to sprint toward the exit. He was fine, though – once you've sung in front of hundreds of thousands of people during the Apocalypse, singing in front of fifty or so people in a local town hall doesn't seem quite as scary.

I watched from the wings as they took to the stage to thunderous applause. It wasn't so long ago that I would have been pretty jealous of their talents. But I knew now that my talent was never going to be singing. Dad liked to put a positive spin on that by saying I was the greatest bad singer he had ever heard. I think he was trying to make me feel better.

At least I had some things to put on the list now:

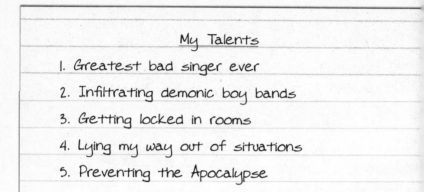

<u>My Talents</u>

1. Greatest bad singer ever
2. Infiltrating demonic boy bands
3. Getting locked in rooms
4. Lying my way out of situations
5. Preventing the Apocalypse

As I watched the band storming it onstage and the look of delight on my parents' faces as they sat in the audience, I thought of another talent to add to the list – helping other people to realize theirs.

The truth was I didn't feel bad about being a terrible singer. How could I when it was the very thing that had helped me to save the world? I didn't know what had happened to Apocalips or the Horsewomen or the Heatherstones or whatever you want to call them, but I knew I couldn't be sure I had seen the last of them. If they ever did return, I'd be waiting for them, ready to do it all over again.

Because saving the world? Now that takes talent.

ABOUT THE AUTHOR

TOM NICOLL has been writing since he was at school, where he enjoyed trying to fit in as much silliness to his essays as he could possibly get away with. When not writing, he enjoys playing video games (especially the ones where he gets beaten by kids half his age from all over the world). He is also a big comedy, TV and movie nerd. Tom lives just outside Edinburgh with his wife, daughter and a cat that thinks it's a dog.

ABOUT THE ILLUSTRATOR

DAVID O'CONNELL cannot sing, play a musical instrument or dance, so would never be in a boy band. In fact, it is far more likely that the Apocalypse will destroy the universe than it is that David will ever agree to sing in public. Luckily for everyone, he is a writer and illustrator, living in London and having fun working on brilliant books like this one.

JOIN **SAM, LEXI** AND **MILO** ON BOTH APOCALYPTIC ADVENTURES.